★ ★ ★

THE MAN WHO SHOT
JOHN WILKES BOOTH

★ ★ ★

KEVIN G. SUMMERS

LITERARY
OUTLAW

FOR
PATTY SUMMERS

YOU SOCKDOLOGIZING
OLD MAN-TRAP

THE TRAGIC PRELUDE

April 1865. The president leaned forward and crossed his arms over the railing of the State Box at Ford's Theatre in Washington City. A slight smile formed at the corners of his mouth. The melancholy that had been assaulting him for most of his presidency, for most of his adult life, was forgotten for the time being. This momentary reprieve from despair came compliments of Harry Hawk, who was giving an absolutely hilarious performance as Asa Trenchard in the play *Our American Cousin.* Abraham Lincoln had desired to see the play ever since it debuted in 1858, but circumstances had not allowed for it until tonight.

Beside the president, to his left, was Mary Todd Lincoln, the First Lady. Though their marriage had been somewhat strained for the past few years, the fires of their love had been rekindled now that the war was all but over. Bobby Lee's surrender six days earlier was the catalyst for this newfound hope. Perhaps now their tribulations were behind them. Two of their children were buried and gone on to whatever awaits us all in the next life, but they still had Robert and Tad. Perhaps there was still time for some joy in their lives. Lincoln felt almost giddy as he watched the performance below. It was blustery outside, but inside Ford's Theatre it was warm, and the president felt like celebrating.

"Don't know the manners of good society, eh?" said Asa Trenchard from the stage as a spattering of laughter rang out from the crowd below.

Lincoln felt his wife's hand slide over his elbow and give him a friendly squeeze. The president turned to look at her, his smile broadening. They had been through so much together, more than any man and woman should be expected to endure. Eddy was buried back in Springfield...

Here my children have been born, and one is buried.

...and Willie was resting in a cemetery over in Georgetown. The president thought about those two sweet boys, and about the town where he had lived for a quarter of a century.

I now leave, not knowing when or whether ever I may return.

Lincoln wanted to return to Illinois. Springfield was home, and when this conflict was over, when his time in the White House was done, he wanted more than anything to visit Eddy back in the Prairie State.

"Well, I guess I know enough to turn you inside out, old gal—" Asa Trenchard said. To the president's right, Henry Rathbone and his fiancé, Clara Harris, were holding hands and chuckling at the scene on stage. Lincoln enjoyed the company of the young couple, though they were not the president's first choice to accompany him and Mary that evening. He had first extended the invitation to U.S. Grant and his wife, but the hero of Appomattox Courthouse had declined.

The president tried to shake the dark feelings that were suddenly bubbling up in him, but it was no use. The peace he felt only seconds before was gone, replaced by a memory that seemed like another lifetime. Back in Springfield, only four years before, the newly elected president bade a somber farewell to the people of his hometown. The words he spoke as he boarded the train that would take him across the country to Washington, and to his fate, came suddenly back to the president:

No one, not in my situation, can appreciate my feeling of sadness at this parting. To this place, and the kindness of these people, I owe everything. Here I have lived a quarter of a century, and have passed from a young to an old man.

I want to go home, the president thought, not for the first time. Washington City is no place for me. I'm exhausted, and what have I done here but send a hundred thousand good boys to their deaths? When I'm cold in the ground that will be my legacy.

Unbeknownst to the presidential party, a man well known at Ford's Theatre was even now crouching outside the door of the State Box, waiting for just the right moment to enter the scene and deliver the most infamous speech of his career as a tragedian. The bodyguard who was supposed to have been watching the door was nowhere to be found.

"—you sockdologizing old man-trap."

The audience burst into uproarious laughter as Asa Trenchard delivered his line. The noise echoed through Ford's Theatre, but the president didn't even crack a smile. He closed his eyes, trying to shake his melancholy. A dream he had had a few nights before flooded back to him from the recesses of his mind. In truth, it had never been buried very deep. The president was standing over a casket in the East Room of the White House. Mourners were all around, their shoulders wracked with sobs.

"Who is dead in the White House?" Lincoln demanded.

"The president," answered a soldier, who stood as an honor guard beside the closed casket, "he was killed by an assassin."

Lincoln opened his eyes as the door to the state booth creaked open behind him. The president sighed, knowing somehow that his time on this world had just run out. A bullet exploded behind his left ear, but strangely, there was no pain. Mary screamed, throwing her arms around her husband's shoulders. She tried to shake the life back into the president; her efforts were in vain. Lincoln slumped forward against the railing as Henry Rathbone struggled against the assassin. The man, his face familiar, drew a dagger from his coat and slashed Rathbone across the forearm. Then the killer climbed onto the railing and leapt to the stage below. His foot caught on a flag that was draped across the front of the booth, causing the assassin to land awkwardly. His leg snapped when he hit the stage, but somehow, through sheer will, John Wilkes Booth was able to stand.

"Sic semper tyrannus!" he shouted. *Thus always to tyrants.* With that, the world slipped into shadow and the president knew no more.

CHAPTER 1

WELCOME TO PARADISE

May 1888. Some women look awfully good in black, and Elizabeth McLarty was one of that kind. She worked afternoons at the offices of the *Paradise Ledger*, doing odd jobs mostly, whatever work needed doing on a particular day. She fetched the mail. She made coffee. She cleaned up after Editor Webb, whose sense of tidiness must have passed on with his wife five years earlier. Webb tried to be fair to the young widow. She certainly didn't have it easy, what with her husband dead and not a soul in town to look after her. More often than not, Joshua Webb found her occupying that place in his mind that had once belonged to his Sarah. She couldn't be more than twenty-four or twenty-five years old, and her husband was two years in the grave.

The widow was standing over Webb's desk with an envelope pinched between the thumb and index finder of her left hand. Not too long ago, she used to wear a ring on that hand, but not anymore. The letter would change everything for Joshua Webb, but he had no way of knowing that. All he knew was that the widow was standing over him, close enough that her perfume filled his nostrils with every breath. It smelled like some emotion he'd almost forgot. Hope, maybe? He couldn't say.

"It's from that lunatic asylum in Topeka," Elizabeth said. "I picked it up from the postmaster on the way over here."

She extended her hand and Webb took the letter. Their fingertips brushed for just a moment, and then the moment was gone. Webb tore off the end of the envelope and slid the letter free.

"Thank you, Miss McLarty," said Webb.

"Please, call me Elizabeth." She smiled, and she was so beautiful that it was almost painful to look at her.

"Just as soon as you start calling me Joshua," said Webb. He hoped that his beard covered the warmth he suddenly felt in his cheeks.

"Is it from the same person? What's his name?"

"Boston Corbett," said Webb. "The man who shot John Wilkes Booth."

"Why does he keep sending you letters?"

"Corbett's a sick man," said Webb. "He was arrested for brandishing a revolver in the Kansas Legislature…been in a sanitarium in Topeka for almost a year now."

"What's he want with you?"

"I don't know. Maybe he thinks I can help him somehow. I don't see how."

Webb unfolded the letter. It was written on a single sheet of vellum in the spidery script of madness. It was addressed to Mr. Joshua Webb, Editor, ℅ The *Paradise Ledger*, Paradise, Colorado. It read:

This is the fourth letter I have
written to you, and your lack of
a response has convinced me that
the tyrants who run this house
of the Devil are intercepting my
mail. I have no earthly idea if

you have even received any of my correspondence, but I pray to God in Heaven that you receive this letter. I fear my time in this life is growing short, and that soon, my knowledge of the truth of President Lincoln's death will be lost forever. If that knowledge means anything to you, then I must urge you to intercede on my behalf.

You may think me mad, but I can assure you that I speak the truth. I can tell you things that would make your heart sink into your bowels. There is a conspiracy at work here, and not the one that cost Mary Surratt her life.

So you think you know the whole story? You don't know anything. You only know what they want you to know, lies and half-truths. But I can tell you the real story. I can tell you what really happened.

But I need your help, and without it you will never know

the real story. Please do what you know is right, Mr. Webb, and stand against the Brotherhood of Deceit.

Humbly yours,
Boston Corbett

"What's it say?" the widow asked.

Webb looked over his glasses at Elizabeth.

Elizabeth McLarty was a handsome woman, with long, red hair that she kept in a tight braid. She was only twenty-two years old when her husband was killed in a freak accident. She bore him no children, and the emptiness of her widowhood radiated out from her until it was almost tangible. Joshua Webb felt it whenever he passed too close to her, and there were times when he considered asking her to be his wife. He was just forty, with a girl at home that he was trying to raise all by himself. Perhaps they could make a family from the shattered pieces of both of their hearts, but not yet.

"He says he knows a secret about the murder of Abraham Lincoln."

A tiny chuckle escaped the widow's lips. "You're not seriously thinking of helping him?" she asked. When Webb didn't answer, an expression of concern darkened the widow's face. "You are? Joshua, are you sure about this?"

"This might be another wild goose chase," said Webb, "but what if it's not? This could be the story of a lifetime."

The widow sighed. "Just like John Brown's ghost? Or that woman who claimed undead slaves slaughtered her family?"

"Listen, Elizabeth, I'll only be away for a few days. Would you mind..."

"Looking in on Abby? Of course. Just promise me you'll be careful."

"I promise."

"She's not going to like it that you're going away again. Maybe you should take her along."

Webb shook his head. "Too dangerous. Besides, she'll be fine. She practically runs the homestead since..." his sentence trailed off. It still hurt to say Sarah's name, even after all these years.

Elizabeth smiled tenderly. "I'll look in on Abby," she said. "I'm sure everything will be fine. So, when are you leaving?"

"Tomorrow," said Webb. "But first, I need to tell Abby."

Nestled amongst the Rocky Mountains, the town of Paradise was founded by Baptist missionaries in the 1860s during the Colorado Gold Rush. They named it Paradise in hopes that it would be a refuge from the rampant sin that was corrupting so many other towns in the untamed western territories. The place seemed like a paradise to Joshua Webb, for a while anyway. It was here that he met Sarah... here that they were wed and brought Abby into the world. But there were shadows at the edges of Paradise, and in time, the shadows enveloped everything.

The town was essentially a single street lined with businesses. Paradise had everything a person could need—a cooper, a blacksmith, a livery, even a doctor's office. At one end of the street was a train depot; at the other, by the river, was the Baptist church. Somewhere in the middle of all those shops, in between *Reynolds Mercantile* and Jake McNair's barber shop, was the little office that housed the town's very own newspaper: the *Paradise Ledger*. Joshua Webb founded the paper in 1869, the year that he left the Army. He met Sarah later that year and they fell in love at first sight. Well, Webb did, it took some persuading on his part to win Sarah's heart, but once he did, he never doubted that she was his and his alone.

Webb exited the clapboard shack that housed his newspaper and went next door to *Reynolds*. Grace Reynolds, the proprietor's wife, sold pies and other baked goods out of the store, and Webb was going to need something to sweeten the news he was about to break to his daughter. Grace was small and frail, an ancient woman who had lost three sons during the War Between the States—one who fought for the Union and two who died for the Confederacy. She smoothed back her white hair and smiled as Webb approached the counter.

"What'll you have?" she asked. Her smile was painful to look upon. It was a mask that barely concealed the sorrow in her heart.

"What do you have today?"

"Strawberry, rhubarb and strawberry-rhubarb."

Webb heard the door open in the background and muffled voices behind him.

"Look who's here?" said a woman's voice in a stage whisper.

"Where you think he's headed this time?

"Pro'lly got another story about the gov'ment controllin' our minds," said another voice. A bark of laughter sounded in the store. Grace Reynolds gave Webb a disapproving look, and then shrugged her shoulders. What could she do about it?

"I feel sorry for his daughter the poor thing," said the first voice.

Sometimes I hate this town, Webb thought. Sometimes I wish Abby and I could just get on a train and go someplace far away–someplace that's never been trod by human feet. But my wife is buried here, and like it or not, I'm going to make my stand here, in Paradise.

"Don't mind them," Grace said. "They wouldn't know good sense if it walked up and bit 'em in the ass." Her smile, for a moment anyway, seemed genuine. "So, what'll it be?"

"Rhubarb," he said. "That's Abby's favorite."

He paid for his pie and then returned to the street. He mounted his horse, an old brown mare whose best years were behind her, and turned her toward home. She was slow and steady, and she got him from place to place, but one day soon, Webb knew that he would find her lying dead in the pasture. That was the way of things, and like it or not, there was nothing he could do about it.

The editor rode out of town and headed north, toward the little homestead he shared with his daughter. Their farm was only a few miles out of town, and Webb used the time to rehearse what he was going to say, knowing all the while that the words would fail him when the time came to break the news. He was going to break Abby's heart, and once again, there was nothing he could do about it.

Abigail Webb loved books more than anything else in the world. When she fell into a story, into a world of fiction, she didn't have to think about her father's work or the way the people in town talked about him when they thought she couldn't hear. When she fell into another world, she didn't have to think about her mother's stone up on the hill, or the sound of the dirt landing on her pine box.

Abby was ten years old when her mother died. Now she was fifteen. Old enough to remember the sad times, but not the joy of knowing a healthy, loving mother. She was barefoot now, sitting in her father's chair with her feet curled beneath her. Her favorite novel was *Jane Eyre*, and she was reading it now for the fourth time.

I care for myself, she read. *The more solitary, the more friendless, the more unsustained I am, the more I will respect myself.*

Abby was small for her age, with straight brown hair that came down almost to her waist when it wasn't up in two braids. She was pale, obscure, plain and little. She had freckles on her cheeks and brown eyes that no one would ever want to gaze into longingly. She was nothing special and she knew it. That's just the way things were.

Abby never heard the sound of approaching hooves. She never heard the door to their little house swing open. She was lost in the world of Charlotte Bronte's creation—in a world where she would have gladly gone to dwell forever.

"Abby?"

She looked up and saw her father standing in the doorway. He held a paper box before him like a gift on Christmas morning. Abby knew right away what that box signified—he was going away again.

Her father was a handsome man, if a bit threadbare. Abby liked to picture him when he was younger, when her mother was still living. His eyes were so full of hope then, now they knew only trouble. They were the vibrant blue of the summer sky after a sudden rain. There were wrinkles at the corners of his eyes, and a pair of glasses perpetually resting on the end of his nose. His hair, once a light brown, was graying at the temples. His beard was almost totally gray now, giving her father the look of a much older man.

"Hi Papa," Abby said.

"How was school today?"

"Fine." Abby was a good student, and she liked her teacher, but she wouldn't say that she enjoyed school. The boys teased her; the girls were worse. "It was fine," she said.

Her father had a sheepish look on his face. He held out the box, offering it to her. "I brought you something," he said. "A rhubarb pie…your favorite."

Abby's look went from the box to her father's face. Their eyes met, and she saw right through him. He knew it, and she knew that he knew it. This was a farce, but still she played along in hopes that things would be different this time. "Thanks, Papa," she said.

"It's your favorite," Webb repeated. His smile was transparent.

"Where'ya headed off to this time?" Abby asked. What was the point of this charade? He was leaving her alone again because some story, some conspiracy or abomination from the gates of Hell was more important than his own flesh and blood. He took her with him one time, shortly after her mother died. Abby was just too young and too fragile to leave at home back then. They traveled all the way to West Virginia, and in her memory, Abby could still recall the strange specter she had seen. Was it a ghost, a real ghost, or a child's imagination? She held on to the hope that these stories that meant so much to her father were real—that he wasn't wasting his life and the precious time they had together in this world chasing after the wind. It almost didn't bother her anymore. Almost.

"Kansas," said her father. "Topeka. There's a story…"

"When will you be home? " Abby said.

Her father's expression darkened, and his eyes went glassy. He stared right through Abby, into a past that was alive but completely untouchable. She knew at once that he was thinking about Mama. What else could he be thinking about? It was like her father had never come back down from the grave after they laid Mama to rest five years before. He was still up there, kneeling in the dirt, sobbing uncontrollably and crying out his wife's name.

"Papa?"

"Sorry," he said, "I was thinking about…"

"Mama?"

"Yeah."

I hate it when he gets like this, Abby thought. He feels guilty for leaving me behind and suddenly he's the one that needs comforting.

Her father's terrible blue eyes turned on her, and it was like he saw her now, really saw her, for the first time. "I ask too much of you Abby," he said. "You take care of the homestead… the animals… and to tell the truth, you take care of me as well."

"Oh Papa," she said. She tried not to cry, but the tears came anyway. Abby threw herself into her father's arms and wept.

"I'm always chasing after my next big story," Webb said, gently petting her hair. "And here you are, growing up so fast I can hardly remember the little girl you used to be. Abby, I'm so sorry. It's just that this story…"

"It's all right," she said. "Just sit down, now. Let's have some pie." She pulled out a chair at their kitchen table and motioned for her father to sit. He did, and Abby set out some dishes and began to slice the pie. She put a big slice on his plate, and even bigger one on hers. The rhubarb filling was tart and sweet and for just an instant, she forgot her anger and her sorrow and her emptiness.

Someone has to be there to take care of him, Abby thought as they ate together in silence. I was just being selfish before. He lost everything when Mama died…he needs me. She reached across the table and took her father's hand.

"When are you leaving?" she asked.

"First thing in the morning. My train leaves at eight." Her father wiped some pie filling from his mustache.

"Will you be careful?"

Webb squeezed her hand. "I will," he said.

I love him so much, Abby thought, but I don't know how to tell him. It's like we can't talk to each other any more.

"When I get back, things are going to be different," said her father.

"Sure they will," Abby said. She wanted to believe it, but she had a sinking feeling that something terrible was about to happen.

★ ★ ★ CHAPTER 2 ★ ★ ★
WIDOWS AND ORPHANS

The train pulled out of the Paradise Depot and headed east, toward Kansas. Webb meant to use his travel time wisely, thus he had pulled every book he had on the Lincoln Assassination out of his personal library. Twenty-three years after the fact, that amounted to six different books on the subject. The well-worn volumes were stacked in the seat beside the editor, each one with tiny slips of paper marking pages containing important passages. The train was thankfully only at about half capacity—otherwise his research would have been considerably more confined.

According to what he read, John Wilkes Booth had not acted alone nor was President Lincoln his only target that tragic day in April 1865. Booth's plan was, apparently, to murder not only Abraham Lincoln but Vice President Andrew Johnson and Secretary of State William Seward as well. He wanted to strike a blow against the Union that would revive the dying Confederacy that he loved so much. So much, that he was willing to kill for it, and so were his conspirators. Unfortunately for Booth, his plan was a disaster. Not only did Seward survive his assault, Johnson wasn't even attacked. For better or for worse, Andy Johnson became the President of the United States, and Lincoln's murder didn't rally the beleaguered rebels. Instead, Abraham Lincoln became a martyr for liberty, and John Wilkes Booth… he became the American Judas.

After shooting the president, Booth spent twelve days on the run before he was finally cornered at Garrett's Farm in Bowling Green, Virginia. There, against the orders of his commanding officer, Booth was gunned down by Sergeant Thomas "Boston" Corbett, a hatter from Troy, New York.

The history books didn't have much to say about Corbett. He was deeply religious, practically a zealot. After killing Booth, Corbett moved out west and eventually became a doorkeeper for the Kansas House of Representatives. A year before, in 1887, Corbett was arrested after waving a revolver at some of the Representatives whom he claimed were heretics. He was thrown in a sanitarium in Topeka, where he'd been writing Webb letters ever since.

Corbett had something he wanted to say, but whatever it might be, Webb had no idea. Was the conspiracy to murder President Lincoln larger than what was commonly known? Perhaps. Booth's co-conspirators, including the widow Mary Surratt, had all been hanged after a public show trial. But was there more... a secret that would turn the nation on its ear if it ever became public?

Webb stared out the window as the train chugged slowly across the grassy plains. He had no idea what he might find in Topeka. He had no idea if he would find anything at all except a lunatic and another wild goose chase.

UPRR
UNION PACIFIC RAILROAD
CABOOSE
14

UNION PACIFIC   RAIL ROAD
BAGGAGE & EXPRESS
UNION PACIFIC
No 73

The selection of books at *Reynolds Mercantile* wasn't exactly poor, they were the only source of literature for miles around, but it was limited. The farmers and cowpokes of Paradise had little use for novels. For Abby Webb, on the other hand, *Reynolds'* small selection was a spring of cool water in a wilderness of ignorance. Hardly a week went by when she didn't find herself picking through the shelves at the mercantile, hoping against hope that Mr. Reynolds had ordered some new books from New York City.

She had no such luck that day, the afternoon after her father left for Topeka. The volumes at *Reynolds* were the same she had perused the week before and the week before that. Melville... Emerson... Whitman... she'd read them all before. Abby was about to leave the store when she heard the bell ring as the shop's door swung open. Two girls entered the Mercantile, and Abby recognized them at once. Nellie Hayes and Alice Burnham—two of the more popular girls at school. Seeing that she would have to pass by them in order to make her escape, Abby opted instead to try and hide in plain sight. She grabbed a book from the shelf and turned her back on the girls.

"Look who it is," said Nellie. Her voice was poison.

"The way she keeps at those books," said Alice, "she'll die an old maid, that's for certain."

The girls laughed, and Abby felt warmth in her cheeks.

"Did you read that crazy story her father printed in the newspaper?"

"Which one?"

"The one about the walking dead. The man's a lunatic."

Abby bit her lip to keep from crying. She tried to read, but the words blurred on the page. She could hear Nellie and Alice coming closer, and she knew in her heart that all of this was a show for her benefit. They hated her, and she had no idea the reason why.

"You know," Alice said, "her father is probably glad that she's so homely."

"Why's that?"

"That way no one will ever want to marry her, and she can take care of him forever."

They laughed outlandishly. Not real laughter, the kind that erupts from your belly and can't be helped. They forced the sound from their pursed lips, each chuckle dripping hatred, the guffaw intended to draw blood.

Abby couldn't take it anymore. She dropped Walt Whitman and shoved past the girls. She burst out of the store with tears streaming down her face. The sound of their laughter trailed after her.

Abby ran without looking where she was going. She didn't see the man in the continental suit standing in front of the store. She was looking at her feet when she collided into the man. It was like hitting a brick wall. He tried to catch her, to break her fall, but he wasn't quick enough. She toppled backward, landing on her backside in the dirty street.

"Now, Child, did you hurt yourself?" The man towered over her, his white suit gleaming in the afternoon sun. He extended a hand up to Abby and she took it without thinking. He pulled her to her feet in one fluid motion.

"Mr. Farnum," Abby said. "I-I'm sorry. I didn't mean…"

"Don't fret, Child," said Jeremy Farnum, the richest man in Paradise. "You have enough to worry about with your… eccentric father. Just be more careful next time." He tipped his hat at Abby and offered a sparkling grin. That terrible smile gave Abby shivers, but she couldn't say why.

"Yes, sir," she said. Her voice trembled.

As he walked past, he paused. "Oh, I hear that your father has been receiving some interesting mail lately. You might want to tell him to tread carefully."

"I-I will," Abby said.

Farnum climbed the steps that led to *Reynolds Mercantile* and disappeared inside the store. Abby, meanwhile, just stood there, watching the man's dust settle into the street.

It was an ordinary day, just like any other, when her husband died. Charles McLarty went out that morning to do the chores, just like he did every morning. He slopped the hogs, fed the chickens and milked Bossy, their cow. He was trimming the horse's hooves when the accident happened. Charles always said that a farrier cost too much, and that Cheyenne was so good, he could do the job himself. And she was good, that was the worst part.

It was in the fall and the turkeys were everywhere that year. Charles had taken a number of birds himself, and he might have gone for more, but he was planning on heading into town that day. Had some business he had to take care of. While other men spent their free time at the saloon, playing cards and drinking, not Charles. He was building them a barn and the mill had some lumber ready for him that day.

The last time Elizabeth saw her husband alive, he had Cheyenne's back foot up in the air. He was clipping the excess hoof when a weapon fired in the nearby woods. It sounded like a canon to Elizabeth, and must have been equally startling to the horse, because she kicked all of sudden. The blow connected squarely with the side of Charles' head, and he went down like a busted sack of feed.

That was it. There was no tearful goodbye like you read in the dime novels. Charles McLarty slumped to the ground and died.

His twenty-two year old widow knelt over him, weeping and screaming in turn, but her tears were in vain. She prayed to sweet Jesus that He would come down and heal her husband. She prayed that He would take her as well, because she couldn't imagine life without her man. When it was apparent that Charles wasn't going to wake up and that Jesus wasn't about to intervene, Elizabeth went into the house and pulled her husband's Sharps Carbine down from over the mantle. She had no idea what she was doing, was acting purely on instinct, when she marched out of the house, placed the end of the rifle against Cheyenne's skull and pulled the trigger. The mare went down screaming and thrashing. It was a foolish thing to do and Elizabeth knew it, but her head wasn't right in that moment. The thought that the beast that killed her love might live while Charles was lying dead in the dirt—that was too much for her.

Charles was gone and she was still here, wandering the little town that had been their home like a ghost in one of Mr. Webb's crazy newspaper stories. The editor had bent over backwards to help her in the weeks after her husband was killed. He gave her a job and comforting words when practically everyone else in Paradise crossed the street when they saw her coming. They acted like it was somehow her fault, that she caused the accident. Elizabeth felt like one of those lepers in the Bible that had to shout "unclean" whenever anyone came near. Didn't they know that she was all alone and afraid? Didn't they know that she sometimes took Charles' Sharps Carbine down from over the mantle and thought about using it on herself?

The widow was working in the offices of the *Paradise Ledger* when she saw Abby Webb come tearing out of *Reynolds Mercantile* . The child wasn't watching where she was going, and she collided into a well-dressed man that could only be Jeremy Farnum. Only a man who didn't give a damn what other people thought about him would go out of the house wearing an outfit like that.

Abby was on the ground and Farnum was helping her to her feet before Elizabeth made it to the door. By the time she crossed the street, Farnum was gone and Abby was standing there, looking on in bewilderment.

"You all right?" asked the widow.

"Yeah. Just didn't watch where I was going," said Abby.

"You sure came out of *Reynolds* in a hurry. Was something wrong?"

Abby shrugged and looked away.

Elizabeth loved Abby like a daughter—like the daughter Charles might have given her if circumstances had been different. She was a sweet child, if a little on the plain side, and the widow saw something of herself in the girl. Clearly something was bothering Abby, and while her father's absence probably had something to do with it, she doubted that was the entirety of the problem.

"Come on," said the widow. "You can tell me."

"It was nothing," Abby said. "Some girls were teasing me."

The widow touched Abby on the arm. "I remember how that feels," she said.

"You do?"

"There was a time when I felt like I didn't have a friend in this world," said Elizabeth.

"But you're so beautiful," Abby said. She looked up at the widow with eyes full of love. *No one has ever told this child that she is beautiful,* Elizabeth thought. *No one has ever taught her how to be a woman.*

"And so are you," Elizabeth said.

Abby blushed and turned away. She was like an orphaned chick unsure on whom it should imprint.

"I hear you're going to stay with me for a few days," she said, "until my father gets back."

"That's right. I'm looking forward to spending some time with you, Abby. It'll be fun."

Abby's smile warmed the widow's heart. "I suppose I should get back to work," Elizabeth said. "I'll see you this afternoon."

"Great," said Abby. "Bye." She walked away, headed for home, and Elizabeth watched her go. Yes, she loved Abby like the daughter she never had, and though she fought to admit it, she had developed a fondness for her father as well. Joshua Webb was a good man, and perhaps, with some persuading, he might consider asking her to be his wife. They could be a family, the three of them, and Elizabeth was young enough that she could give him another child.

Smiling, the widow returned to the offices of the *Paradise Ledger*. She had no idea that man dressed all in white was watching her from a window of *Reynolds Mercantile* .

"Tell him to tread carefully."

Abby was hanging wet laundry on a line in her front yard, but all she could think about was her encounter with Jeremy Farnum earlier that day. The richest man in town seemed so smug, and what did he mean about interesting mail?

She pinned one corner of a sheet to the line and was working on pinning the other without dropping it in the grass when she heard hoof beats in the distance. Abby looked through an opening in the laundry and saw a man on horseback riding toward the house.

Abby kept on with her work because it was her way. Every shirt or apron she hung up now would be one more she wouldn't have to hang later. She worked until the man drew up his horse right in front of her.

He wore a burgundy sack suit, slightly worn, and a white Stetson cocked back on his head. His hair was golden, and his face looked as clean as if he'd just shaved. He wore a gun belt under his coat, and Abby could see a holster resting on hip... resting within easy reach.

"Good afternoon, little sister," he said. "Recon I could trouble you for a drink of water?"

"What? Yes. Certainly." Abby blushed as he looked her over. She went to the well and began to draw his water. She was suddenly conscious of the braids in her hair and how they made her look like a little girl. Mr. Farnum's comments about her father flew out of her mind like chickens trying to escape the coop. She looked up at the stranger who had dismounted and was now standing beside his horse. He was smiling at Abby, watching every move that she made. His eyes made Abby feel almost uncomfortable, but she kind of liked it at the same time. And she had to admit that he was a handsome fellow.

Abby returned to the stranger and handed him a dipper of water. The tips of their fingers brushed one another as the man took the cup. He drank it greedily, not seeming to care when some of the water dribbled onto his suit.

"Thank you, Miss…" he said.

"Webb," said Abby. "Abigail Webb. Y-you can call me Abby."

The stranger smiled. "Well, thank you, Abby. My name is Francis Avery, but you can call me Frank."

"Where are you headed?" Abby said. "I haven't seen you around these parts before."

"I'm new in town," said Frank. "Gonna be doing some work for a Mr. Jeremy Farnum."

"Oh. I just saw Mr. Farnum this morning. What kind of work are you going to be doing?"

Frank smiled. "This and that," he said. "Say, are all the girls in these parts as pretty as you?"

Abby blushed and turned her head.

"Tell me about yourself," said Frank. "Where are your parents?"

"My father is a newspaperman. He's off in Kansas working on a story. My mother… she passed away."

"I'm so sorry to hear that."

He reached out to her, as if he were going to caress her cheek, and at that moment, the door to the house banged open and the Widow McLarty appeared in the doorway. She didn't say a word, but Abby could feel her presence and her gaze from across the lawn.

"Who's that?" Frank whispered.

"Elizabeth McLarty," said Abby. "She's staying with me while my Papa… my father is out of town. "

The widow was walking across the lawn now, and Abby knew that she was going to run this sweet young man off the property. She wished that their meeting didn't have to end like this, but what could she do?

McLarty stepped between Abby and Frank. She glared at the girl, challenging her to say anything, and then turned to the stranger. Abby bit her lip to keep from putting her foot in her mouth. Elizabeth was in charge here and there was nothing Abby could do about it. Was there?

"What do you want here, young man?" said the widow.

"Just a drink of water, Ma'am," Frank said. "This pretty young lady was nice enough to fetch it for me."

"You've had your drink," said McLarty. "Now it's time to be moving on."

Frank Avery nodded at Abby, and then mounted his horse. "Farewell, Ladies," he said. "I hope to make your acquaintance again."

He rode off, kicking up a cloud of dust in his wake. Abby and Elizabeth watched him go, riding toward town at full gallop.

"That boy is trouble incarnate," said the widow as Frank disappeared over the horizon.

Abby hoped he was right—hoped that she would see him again soon.

★ ★ ★ CHAPTER 3 ★ ★ ★
AN INCIDENT AT TOPEKA STATE HOSPITAL

The Free State Hotel in Topeka, Kansas was quiet that night in the spring of 1888. The rough crowds, the kind of folk that frequented saloons and brothels, steered clear of the establishment. It wasn't their sort of place. It was May 26th, four days after Joshua Webb left Paradise.

The editor was sitting on his bed in his room on the second floor of the hotel. His feet ached, his back ached, and he wanted more than anything to be back at his little homestead with Abby. He wanted Elizabeth McLarty by his side, and if she would have him, he wanted her in his bed and in his life. Webb would have done anything for one more minute with Sarah, but that was never going to happen. She was gone... gone over to the far side banks of the Jordan, and he would never again lay eyes on her this life. But he had a daughter to raise and he was still a man. A man needs a woman, and Abby needed a mother. The Widow McLarty could fit both of those roles. Fit them right nicely too.

The room was barren with just a bed and a night-stand and a piss pot. Somewhere outside, Webb heard the sound of laughter floating on the night air. He took off his boots.

Before this most recent letter from Boston Corbett, back when the madman first started his long, weird correspondence, Webb sent a telegram to the military administrator of the Topeka Asylum. His response was that Boston Corbett was not allowed any unauthorized visitors.

Webb lifted his leather valise and placed it on the bed. He opened the bag and revealed a Federal Army coat inside. Webb had worn this uniform back when he served his country during the Indian Wars. After the nightmare at Washita, he resigned his commission and moved to Paradise. The uniform had rested in a drawer ever since, moldering away like John Brown's body in that song some of the old soldiers liked to sing. The editor loosened his tie and unbuttoned his vest.

If Corbett is telling the truth, Webb thought, if there is some kind of conspiracy here, there's no way a reporter is getting anywhere near the asylum.

The editor removed his trousers and replaced them with blue wool trousers he once wore in the Army. They were a bit snug, but just a bit. He fastened a belt around his waist, his fingers tracing the engraved letters U.S. on the buckle.

That leaves me with just one option, he thought. I have to become someone else.

The Topeka State Hospital was a six-story monstrosity on the outskirts of the city. It had pointed towers like a castle in a children's storybook, and a rounded, sweeping porch littered with madmen in rocking chairs. The architecture required to construct such a building was impressive, there was no doubt, and the building gave off a sense of something dark and terrible—something evil. Webb stood before the

terrible place, itching all over in his blue Federal uniform.

Haven't been a praying man since Sarah died, he thought. *Maybe it's time to reconsider my agnosticism.*

Wood creaked beneath his feet as the editor climbed the steps onto the huge porch. A man in loose-fitting clothes was rocking at the top of the steps. Was it Corbett? He was pale and thin, but he didn't match the photographs Webb had seen of Booth's killer. This wasn't his man, but wouldn't that have been a simple thing?

"Howdy," said the inmate.

"Good evening," said Webb.

"You seen my girl?" the man asked.

"No, sir," said Webb.

"She's awful pretty," said the man. "Yellow hair and big tits, you couldn't miss her."

"I think I would have remembered if I saw her," Webb said.

"You see her," said the man, "you tell her her daddy wants her to come home, you here?"

"I'll do that," said Webb.

Webb went to the front door and turned the knob. He stepped inside and was immediately struck by the smell of urine. There was an old man in a red union suit standing in the foyer. His back was to Webb, but by the smell and the sound, the editor knew at once what was happening. The old man was pissing on the floor. He smiled at Webb as he walked by.

"Mr. Taylor," came a harsh voice, "what in the world do you think you're doing?"

A large woman brushed past Webb on her way to the old man. She was thick with fat and muscle, and her brown hair was pulled back off her round neck into a severe bun. She grabbed the old man with one hand and twisted his arm behind his back. His cock dangled from the front of his union suit, but the woman paid it no mind. She paused after forty seconds or so, as if she just noticed Webb for the first time.

"Can I help you Mister…?"

Webb looked from the man to the nurse, trying to hide his disgust. "Hodge," he said. "Lieutenant Lewis Hodge, 7th Cavalry. I'm here to speak with one of your inmates—Sergeant Thomas Corbett."

The woman glared at him as her beefy fingers sunk deeper into the old man's arm. He wailed in agony, but if she noticed, she didn't give any indication. "Second floor," she said. "Down at the far end of the hall."

"Thank you, ma'am."

Webb mounted a curved stairway that he assumed was built into one of the towers he'd noticed outside. There were small windows built into the walls, and daylight and poured in, casting harsh shadows on the walls. When he reached the top, he found himself at the head of a long, narrow hallway lined with closed doors. There was a large window at the far end of the hall. He thought about the real Lewis Hodge as he walked slowly down the corridor. The man was a Captain and Webb's superior back when he served in the Army, but a Lieutenant's uniform was all that the editor had.

They were on the Washita River in the fall of '68, serving in the 7th Cavalry under George Armstrong Custer. Webb and Hodge were part of a company of soldiers that raided a village where the outlaw Black Kettle was believed to be hiding. Their orders were to capture the women and children, but that isn't what happened. One of the women resisted and it was like a demon came forth out of the depths of Hell. The soldiers, Webb included, slaughtered everyone—men, women, children—it didn't matter.

When the murdering was over, Webb was ashamed of what he had done. Hodge said that it didn't matter, that they were just following orders, but Webb was never the same after that. He resigned his commission in the Army and moved to Paradise. Other than shooting the occasional coyote or chicken-stealing varmint, Webb had never touched a gun again.

The editor reached the end of the hall and the door that the nurse downstairs had indicated. He rapped his knuckles lightly on the door, and heard slight movement coming from the other side. Here we go, he thought as he turned the handle. The door swung inward, revealing a room cast in heavy shadows. The curtains were drawn, blocking most of the sunlight from entering the room. There was a man sitting in a rocking chair in the center of the room. He had a blanket wrapped all around him, and he was hugging it to his chest like a lover. His long, dark hair fell all around his face in an unkempt, greasy mess. He wore a scraggly beard that grew in patches on his cheeks. Even in the miniscule light, Webb could see the man's eyes moving, darting back and forth as he took in the Army officer that had just stepped into his room.

"Mr. Corbett?" said Webb.

"Who's asking?"

"My name is Joshua Webb. I got your letter."

Corbett rocked gently in his chair. He said nothing. Webb looked around in the darkness. The room was almost bare: a bed; a chamber pot; the rocking chair. There was a cross on the wall with a bloody, dying Jesus crucified upon it.

"I've come to learn the truth," said Webb.

"What is truth?"

Great, Webb thought. He's quoting Pilate. This is going to be bad.

Downstairs, on the main level of the State Hospital, the duty nurse stepped into the office of Colonel Josiah Faylen, the Army Liaison Officer. His hair was black and thinning to a near point atop his head. He wore thick burnsides that met under his nose. Faylen was fifty years old and a veteran of Gettysburg. He was there when Robert E. Lee surrendered to the Army of Northern Virginia. He was there when Joshua Chamberlain ordered his men to carry arms as a show of respect to the rebels. Faylen had done as he was ordered on that day in 1865 though he thought it was foolishness at the time. He thought so still, but you followed orders, and that's all there was to it.

"What is it?" he said as the nurse leaned into his office. She had a smug look on her face that Faylen would have liked to wipe away. She didn't like him much, and as far as he was concerned, the feeling was mutual.

"I'm sorry to bother you," she said, "but I thought you'd like to know there's a soldier here asking about Sergeant Corbett."

Faylen's eyes narrowed. "What'd you tell him?"

The nurse smiled. "I told him where to find Corbett, of course. It's not my job to get in the middle of you Army men." Her eyebrows flared at the end of her words, and once more Faylen was tempted to strike the woman. He had never married, and working in such close proximity to this harpy, he was thankful to his younger self for choosing to remain a bachelor.

"Son of a bitch," he muttered as he stood. He retrieved a revolver from his desk drawer and loaded it. His assignment to this hellhole was, primarily, to make sure that nothing happened to Corbett. Generals and Senators were all interested in the man, though Faylen had no idea why that was. Boston

Corbett was a lunatic, and even if he had done the world a favor by putting a bullet in John Wilkes Booth, nothing was going to change that fact. "Tell the boys to meet me upstairs," he said to the nurse.

"Colonel?"

"And tell them to come armed." The colonel left his office and headed toward the stairs. If someone was up there with Corbett, they hadn't cleared it with him. That meant they were either an impostor, or an assassin. Either way, he meant to find out.

Webb sat on the bed because it was the only place to sit. It was unmade, with the meager covers bunched at the foot of the bed. The sheets were filthy, and Webb felt his skin crawl the moment that his pants touched the fabric. "You said if I helped you, you'd tell me the truth about the Lincoln Assassination," he said. "Well, here I am."

Boston Corbett rocked back gently in his chair. He was positioned in such a way that his back was mostly turned to the editor.

"You've come to get me out of here," he said. There was a matter-of-factness in his voice that Webb found troubling.

"This institution is guarded by the Federal Army. Getting you out of here isn't as simple as it sounds."

"Nevertheless," Corbett said, "that is why you have come, is it not?" Webb caught a slight, half smile in the strange man's profile. "You wear their uniform," he said. "You have spun deceptions to get this far. You would not have done these things if you had no plan of escape."

Webb's fingers twisted absently at the point of his beard. He needed a trim. "I came here to talk with you, not help you escape. The uniform was enough to get me through the door, but…"

Corbett cut him off mid-sentence. "Are you a man of faith, Mr. Webb?"

The editor thought about his wife writhing in agony as the smallpox slowly took her. He had been a praying man in those days, a man that thought that if he prayed hard enough his God might reach down from Heaven and heal his wife. That God never answered, however, and when Sarah died, so did his faith.

"Not particularly," Webb said.

"Jesus said unto him, if thou canst believe, all things are possible to him that…"

His words were cut off by a crash as the door to Corbett's room was kicked open. A man in an Army uniform stood in the door, brandishing a pistol. Webb jumped up immediately, but Corbett just kept rocking in his chair as if nothing out of the ordinary had happened.

"I don't know what this is all about," said the man with the gun, "but both of you are coming down to my office where we're going to have a little talk." The soldier took a step back and gestured with his pistol that they should follow.

Webb and Corbett shared a look, but if Booth's assassin was troubled by this turn of events, he gave no indication.

"Come on," said the soldier. "Get moving."

Boston Corbett arose from his rocking chair. He was so thin that his clothes looked like they might fall right off of him. He moved slowly toward the door, his eyes never leaving the colonel.

I should be a novelist, Webb thought, like that Mark Twain. My career in journalism causes me nothing but trouble.

They stepped into the hall, and immediately noticed a group of soldiers at the far end, near the stairs. They were armed, but not one had his weapon drawn. In that moment, when the two groups first saw one another, Corbett exploded into motion. He spun around and delivered a swift punch to the colonel's throat.

It happened so fast that Webb didn't even have time to react. He watched as the colonel gasped for breath, his mouth opening and closing like a fish snatched from the water.

Corbett was behind the colonel now, and had relieved the man of his revolver. He leveled the weapon at the oncoming soldiers and fired. Webb stood there watching, unable to move until Corbett turned to him and calmly said, "Get down."

Webb dropped to the floor as the soldiers sprayed lead at Corbett. A bullet grazed his shoulder, but he didn't even seem to notice. He fired again and again until every soldier was dead. There was nothing for Webb to do but watch in awe. It's like Washita all over again, he thought. Only this time it's U.S. Soldiers being slaughtered.

The colonel slumped to the ground, his body riddled with bullets. In a matter of seconds, the firefight was over. The corridor was filled with looming silence and the acrid smell of gunsmoke.

Webb sat up on his knees and looked up at Corbett. He wore the same calm expression on his face, as if this were all perfectly ordinary. There was a nasty-looking wound on his right shoulder—his shirt was soaked in blood.

"You're wounded," said Webb.

Corbett looked at the wound as if noticing it for the first time. "It's nothing," he said.

Webb stared down the hallway, at the dead and dying soldiers. Corbett, meanwhile, was inspecting the colonel's body. He removed a box of ammunition from the man's belt pouch.

"You killed them all," said Webb. He still couldn't believe how quickly this had happened.

"I sent them to the Lord," Corbett said, "as they would have done for me. And you, Mr. Webb."

"That doesn't make it any easier."

Corbett stuffed the revolver into his belt and began to examine the window at the end of the hall. Several panes were gone, ruined by the firefight from a few moments before. "Come on, Mr. Webb," he said. "It's time we fled this place of death." With that, he kicked out the remaining panes and all of the wooden framing. The assassin's assassin climbed through the window and onto the roof of a covered porch.

After a minute, Webb followed him onto the porch. They climbed down the porch's supports and reached the ground a minute later. As the awe of what had happened inside wore off, the Topeka State Hospital was suddenly alive with sounds. Weeping... screaming... shouts from someone that had been brave enough or foolish enough to check on the colonel and his men.

What is truth? Webb thought as he followed Corbett toward the stables. *I've chased that question all over this country. Sacrificed my reputation for it, and now here I am. What is truth? That's what I aim to find out.*

CHAPTER 4

BLEEDING KANSAS

It was dusk on the prairie outside of Topeka, Kansas. Webb and Corbett were closing in on the city, having ridden the long way around in hopes to confuse the trail for any soldiers that might have followed them from the State Hospital. Of course, the trail of blood that stretched out behind them would eventually reveal their location no matter how well they hid. Corbett was wounded, his shirt a bloody mess, and risky or not, if he didn't see a doctor soon he was going to die.

"You okay?" said Webb. The question was rhetorical, but what else could he say? In a minute or an hour, Corbett was going to fall off of his horse and when that happened, all bets were off.

"He maketh me… to lie down in… green pastures…" Corbett said. He mumbled, forcing each word through his gritted teeth.

"That wound in your shoulder is starting to worry me something terrible," said Webb.

Thus far, Booth's killer hadn't said a word about the conspiracy to murder Abraham Lincoln. That was the entire reason Webb had traveled the five hundred miles between Paradise and Topeka. And if Corbett dropped dead from a gunshot wound, all of that would be for nothing. Webb was starting to wonder if he'd been had. And after the debacle back at the hospital, Webb realized that he might well meet his fate at the end of a rope.

"Don't' fret f'r me…Mis-ter Webb," Corbett said. "Y-you're… concern… should… the… Society."

"This Society," said Webb, "who are they? Did they have something to do with the Lincoln Assassination? What can you tell me about them?

Corbett's face took on an expression of near serenity as he sank into the lake of his memories.

"There are… three infernal organizations constantly vying for power… in this nation," he said.

"The Freemasons are by far the most... prevalent, and the most powerful, of the societies that secretly control our country. Washington. Franklin. Monroe. Jackson. Every one of them was a Freemason. When Lincoln was murdered, it was a Mason, Andrew Johnson, who ascended to the White Throne... of the Republic.

"Though they reaped the reward," he continued, "and the balance shifted once more to their favor, it was not the Freemasons... who were responsible for Lincoln's death. The Skull and Bones Society, based out of Yale University, has gained great prominence in recent years. Senators and Chief Justices and the leaders of industry have all consigned their souls to this cursed fraternity, but their star has not yet fully risen. In time, perhaps, they will wield the sword... and the gavel with the precision of the Masons, but not yet.

"It is the Society of the Cincinnati, those Luciferian dogs, who are responsible for the death of Abraham Lincoln."

"The Society of the Cincinnati?" Webb repeated. He searched his own mind for mentions of the organization. Something about the Revolution came to mind, but he couldn't say what exactly.

"The Society was founded by Alexander Hamilton and Henry Knox at the close of the American Revolution, and was intended as a gentleman's club for former officers who wanted to protect their newly won liberty. It included George Washington and twenty-three signers of the Constitution."

"Washington?" Webb said. "I thought you said he was a freemason."

Corbett nodded enthusiastically, and the motion sent him into a fit of coughing. "Yes," he managed. He smiled in spite of his obvious pain, as if this somehow made sense to the editor.

"You're telling me that George Washington was a member of both organizations?" Webb asked.

Corbett nodded. "He was... a man of great... charisma."

"He played both ends against the middle," said Webb.

Corbett nodded and moved on, as if there was nothing more to say about the founder of the nation. "Jefferson Davis and his... Confederacy answered to the Society," he said, "and for a time it seemed that the balance would shift in their favor."

"What happened?"

"The end of the war meant the end of their control," Corbett said. "Their only hope was to reignite the fighting. They trained Wilkes for years... as a failsafe. Lincoln's death might have ended the war, or might have revived the defeated Southern spirit once Lee surrendered. Obviously... the plan failed. Aghhh.

Webb looked at Corbett and knew at once that his time was almost up. "Dammit," he said, "we need to get you to a doctor."

There was no use in waiting any longer. Corbett was going to die unless he saw a physician at once. Even then he still might perish, and with him all the knowledge of this conspiracy. Perhaps the Army was waiting for them in town, ready to seize them both the moment they appeared. But perhaps, if luck was on their side, they would make it. Once again, Joshua Webb considered saying a prayer to the God whom he had abandoned. Once again, he decided against it.

They kicked their horses into a gallop and raced through the tall prairie grass. Topeka was close, and if fortune was on their side, they would make it before Corbett's injury overcame him.

There was a doctor near Webb's hotel in Topeka; he noticed the man's sign when he got off the train. The clinic was located in a fine house with a wraparound porch and a half-dozen windows on the second story. Webb tied up the horses, helped Corbett to the ground, and together they approached the clinic. Corbett nearly tripped as he tried to step up onto the porch, but Webb caught him.

"Steady," said the editor. "We're gonna get you some help."

The shingle beside the front door read: R. MASSEY, M.D. Webb knocked lightly, hoping that the doctor was still awake. An old man with a kind face opened the door a moment later.

Doc Massey was a venerable fellow with a face as hairless as that of a child. He squinted into the darkness at the two strangers standing on his porch. One was wearing an Army uniform, and the other was clearly injured.

"Sir," said Webb, "this man is grievously wounded. Can you help him?"

The doctor's eyes went from Webb to Corbett and then lit up.

"Boston?" he said. "Boston Corbett, is that you?"

Corbett nodded and groaned something that might have been an affirmation.

"Sweet Jesus," said Massey, "get him inside before he dies out here."

Webb helped his injured companion through the door and into Doc Massey's parlor. The walls were papered with a yellow-gold print, and the furniture was of fine construction. Massey was clearly a man of wealth, and obviously someone that was familiar with his new friend. What that might mean for this story, Webb couldn't say.

They followed Massey to a table in the center of the room, and Webb helped Corbett up onto the oak structure. The doc, meanwhile, was lighting oil lamps stationed throughout the room. When the light was sufficient for the old man to do his work, he approached the table.

"What the hell happened to him?" said the old man when he caught sight of Corbett's bloody shoulder.

"I don't know," Webb said. "I found him like this outside of town. I think he was ambushed by des- perados. They even took his clothes. It was a good thing I came along when I did." It was the least plau- sible story Joshua Webb had ever told, and that was saying something considering the typical content of his newspaper, but it was the best he could come up with on such short notice.

Doc Massey gave Webb a long, doubtful look. "Don't lie to me," he said. "I know for a fact that Boston is supposed to be locked up over at the State Hospital. It was in every damned paper in town when he pointed a gun at that congressman. Son of a bitch probably deserved it, but that's no matter."

Webb began to speak, but he couldn't get a word in edgewise. "Now either something happened to him at the hospital and you've brought him here because the doctor over there is a complete jackass, or something strange is going on here. Now which is it? Boston, you want to tell me what's going on?"

Corbett stared through the doctor, his eyes devoid of light or intelligent thought. He looked like a wild animal that had been killed and stuffed and mounted up on the wall.

"He escaped, sir," said Webb. "I helped him escape."

"And someone shot him while you were trying to get out?"

Webb nodded. "Something like that."

"This man is an American hero," said Doc Massey. "He put that yellow bastard Booth in the grave where he belongs. Ain't right for him to be locked up in a place like that, and I don't care what he did."

"Sir," said Webb, "I believe that the Army is going to come looking for Boston here. We need to be moving out as soon as possible. Tonight even. Can you help him?"

"I'll do what I can for him," said the doc. He retrieved a pair of pliers from a drawer, and set about boiling some water to sterilize them. "I take it you're not really with the Army," he said as he waited for the pot to boil.

"No sir," said Webb. "Not for a long time."

"Did you fight in the war?"

"No," said Webb. "Not your war anyway. I fought the Indians with General Custer."

"You seen any blood? Any killing?" said Massey.

Webb nodded. "More than I cared to, sir," said Webb. He thought about Washita, and the bodies of the women and children. Sometimes he could still hear their cries when it got very quiet in the night.

"I don't know if you're squeamish," said the Doc, "but you may want to step outside for a few minutes."

Webb looked from Massey to Corbett. There was nothing he could gain by watching what was about to happen. He'd seen it all during his time in the Army, and if he could go the rest of his life without hearing another man scream, that would be just fine with him.

"If you'll excuse me," he said, "I'll just wait outside."

"Fine," said the Doc. "That's just fine. You can move your horses to my barn out back. I don't think you're gonna be going anywhere anytime soon."

Webb did as he was instructed, unbridling the horses and leaving them in a couple of empty stalls in the barn. When he was done, he went back to his hotel and changed clothes. There was a small mirror in the room, and when Webb took a look at his reflection, his eyes were drawn immediately to his beard. He was on the run now, and there was one thing he could do in a matter of minutes that would drastically alter his appearance. His fingers went to his beard, stroking it regretfully, like a man that knows he has to shoot a favorite dog.

When he returned to the clinic, clean-shaven and wearing his civilian clothes once more, Doc Massey was waiting for him on the front porch. "I don't know if he's going to live," he said. "Don't know if he's gonna have to lose that arm. Equal chance of either if you want the truth."

Webb nodded. "I thank you," he said. "How much do I owe you?"

The doc shrugged. "Boston's a hero," he said. "This one is on the house."

"You sound as if you've met him before," Webb said. "When we first arrived on your doorstep."

"We attended services together," said Massey. "That is to say, we both attended the same church. Do you know the Lord, sir?"

Webb looked away. "I do," he said.

"Something tells me that you and He aren't exactly on speaking terms. Am I wrong?"

"No, sir," said Webb. "You're not wrong."

"The Lord has His hand on Mr. Corbett," said Massey. "You think about that, and you'll know I'm right."

"I will," said Webb. "Now, I'd like to see him."

"That's fine," said the doc. "He's upstairs, resting. But you don't bother him long, do you hear me?

"Yes, sir."

Corbett was resting in a four-poster bed in an upstairs room of Doc Massey's home. His shoulder was wrapped in white clothes that were slowly turning red. He appeared calm, as if the agony of only a few minutes before had happened to someone else. The man who shot John Wilkes Booth stared at a blank wall across the room from his bed, his eyes completely vacant.

Webb pulled a wooden chair up beside the bed and sat down. He was running out of time. Before long, the Army was going to come looking for their escaped prisoner and his accomplice. Trouble was riding high in the saddle and headed for Topeka. If there was any hope of uncovering the truth, this was the time.

"I'm sorry to bother you while you're recovering," said Webb, " but I was hoping you could tell me your story."

Corbett said nothing.

"None of this worked out like I planned," said Webb. "I figured that we would talk at the hospital... that my story would cast new light on the Lincoln assassination. I had no idea that you were going to kill those guards. I never wanted any part of murder."

Still Corbett said nothing.

Webb was beginning to wonder if the man were simply insane—if all of this was a terrible jest. "I have a daughter back home in Paradise," said Webb. "If I had known what you were capable of... I should have never come here."

Corbett turned to him at last, and finally Webb saw light return to the man's eyes. "I was born Thomas Corbett in 1832," he said. The editor quickly did the math in his head and placed Corbett at fifty-six years old.

My family moved to New York when I was seven," Corbett continued. "It was there that I fell in love with a girl named Susan. We married in 1854, but she died in childbirth."

Webb bowed his head as he thought about Sarah. In the years since she was gone, there wasn't a day that went by when he didn't think about her. He loved her now as he always had, as he always would. When his thoughts turned to Elizabeth McLarty, what it would be like to hold her in his arms, it felt like he was somehow betraying Sarah. She would have wanted him to be happy, not to be alone, but that didn't matter. "I'm sorry," he said. "I lost my wife as well."

If he heard, Corbett offered no sympathy. "Devastated," he said, "I turned to the bottle for comfort. In the depths of my depravity, awaiting death, the Society found me. The masters of the Brotherhood became my gods, and I was to them a pistol to be fired whenever they saw fit. They conditioned me to kill without mercy, to accept pain without complaint, and above all else, to follow orders without question. It was there that I first met Wilkes."

"Wait a minute," said Webb. "You're telling me that you knew John Wilkes Booth before the assassination?"

Corbett nodded. "We trained together," he said. "We were apprentices..."

Just then, the door swung open and Doc Massey stepped into the room. "Excuse me," he said, "but I was just over at the saloon and I overheard something that might interest the both of you."

Webb and Corbett exchanged a look. "What's that?" said Webb.

"There's soldiers in town. They're down to the sheriff's office right now."

Damn, Webb thought. I was hoping we'd have enough time to get out of town before the Army caught up to us. "Thank you, Doc," he said, trying to sound calm.

"If you two are in trouble," said Massey, "I'll do whatever I can to help."

Webb and Corbett exchanged a look.

"If those soldiers find out that Boston is here," said Webb, "he's going to die."

"Die? Because of an escape attempt?"

"There's something larger going on here," said Webb. "I can't say what it is just now, because I don't fully understand it myself. But dark forces are at work to silence this man, and that's why I need to get him out of Topeka."

Massey nodded. "How can I help?"

"If the soldiers come around, I need you to divert them. Tell them that we went south. Tell them that we were planning to go to Texas."

"I can do that," said Massey. "They might not believe me, but..."

A terrible banging sound filled the house, and Webb knew at once that he was too late. The Army was here, and in minutes, this exercise in futility was going to be over.

"Doc Massey," said whoever was banging on the door. "Richard Massey, we need to talk to you."

"This fellow needs plenty of rest," Massey said. "I'd hate to see that wound get infected."

"We have to leave," said Webb. "Is there a way out the back?"

"Down the hall, on the left," said the Doc. "The window in that back room overlooks another porch. You should be able to climb down and make it over to my barn."

"What are you going to do?"

"I'll stall them as long as I can," Massey said. "Now you two be quiet and get the hell out of here." The doctor left the room and closed the door behind him. Webb heard his footfalls on the stairs, and he knew that he had only a matter of minutes before this entire situation collapsed in on itself.

"The army is here to arrest you," Webb said. "We have to get out of here right away."

"How?"

Webb sighed deeply. "Doc Massey is going to stall them, but that will only buy us a couple of minutes at most."

"Perhaps we should rely on Providence," said Corbett. "The Lord will protect us if our faith is strong enough."

"Or maybe the Lord wants us to skedaddle on out of here," Webb said. "Come on."

Webb helped Corbett out of bed, and the two men moved as quickly as they could down the corridor. They walked in silence, knowing that the sound of a creaking board might signal the Army that someone was attempting to flee. They heard only scattered bits of the conversation downstairs, but it was enough to eliminate any doubts in Webb's mind about the reason for the late night visit.

"...State Hospital..."

"...murdered..."

"...accomplice..."

Webb pushed his charge a little harder, knowing that the next few seconds might make all the difference. They reached the room at the end of the hall and entered. There was a moment when Webb feared that the door might be locked, but the handle turned easily and made not a sound as the door swung open on its hinges. They stood in the darkness of the back room, the only light was that of the moon outside, and Webb could nearly taste their freedom. Corbett leaned against the wall as Webb reached for the window. It wouldn't budge.

"Oh no," said Webb as he strained against the window. It held fast. At that moment, as he forced every bit of his strength into his fingertips, he heard the sound of footsteps on the stairs. It sounded like a herd of buffalo, or a small army, was climbing up to the second floor of the building.

"They're coming," said Corbett. "We'll have to fight them."

"No," said Webb. "No more killing."

Corbett started to speak, but Webb cut him off.

"We're not fighting them," he said. "We're getting out of here and I'm going back to Paradise to be with my girl. Do you understand me?" His eyes flared with passion, and in that instant, they both knew that Webb would abandon Corbett then and there if it came to it. Hopefully, it would not. "Come on," he said, "help me with this window."

Corbett moved over beside Webb and, using his good hand, added his strength to the struggle. After several agonizing seconds, the window finally budged. Unfortunately, it sounded a loud creak that echoed in the silent room.

"Hurry," Webb ordered. He practically shoved Corbett through the opening. The man who shot John Wilkes Booth crawled out onto the porch roof and then helped the editor out into the night. They spider-walked across the roof until they reached the edge nearest the barn. Webb climbed down first and then helped Corbett as he attempted to scale the structure's supporting poles with one arm. Corbett was almost to the ground when a soldier appeared in the window above them.

"You there," he shouted, "halt in the name of the United States Army."

Webb pulled Corbett the last few feet to the ground, and they toppled over onto the grass. The soldier was shouting for his comrades and climbing out onto the roof as Webb pulled Corbett to his feet. "Run!" he shouted.

They ran, abandoning the horses that were even now waiting for them in the barn. They could not hope to saddle their mounts and escape in time, and so they fled on foot. Their only hope was to lose the soldiers in the darkness of the Kansas countryside. It was a slim hope at best, but perhaps the Lord was on their side after all. Webb had to count on that because it was all he had. All that mattered to him now, even more than revealing the truth about Abraham Lincoln's assassination, was getting back to Abby. She needed him, Webb could sense that somehow. She needed him and once again, he wasn't there for her.

Back in Paradise, the sun was setting on the Webb homestead that same evening. The chores were done, and whatever work remained unfinished would have to remain until morning. Abby had made a fine dinner of roasted chicken and mashed potatoes, and she was looking forward to spending some time with Elizabeth McLarty, one of her favorite people in the world. The widow had a wicked sense of humor, and even though she would never replace her mother, Abby liked the way that her father became so animated whenever the handsome woman came around. They had just sat down to supper, and after a hard day of work, Abby was looking forward to a hearty meal. She bowed her head and Elizabeth did the same.

"Bless us, Lord," said the widow, "and these thy gifts which we are about to receive from thy bounty. Through Christ, our Lord. Amen."

"Amen," said Abby.

Elizabeth carved the chicken as Abby served them each a heaping spoon of potatoes. She sprinkled salt over her meal, and then dipped a piece of meat into the potatoes.

"Jeremy Farnum stopped into the paper today," Elizabeth said. "I don't like that man."

Abby snickered. "I know what you mean," she said. "There's something about him. He just rubs me the wrong way."

"Me too," Elizabeth said. "He was asking a lot of question about your father. Where's he's been the past few days, that sort of thing. I didn't say a word except that he was away on business."

A memory of her last encounter with Farnum flashed in Abby's mind, and considering the emotion it had provoked, she was amazed that she had forgotten. "He said something the other day about some mail that came to Papa. He said that he should tread carefully."

Elizabeth stiffened.

"Is something wrong?" Abby asked.

"How would he know about your father's mail?" said the widow.

"I don't know. You don't think the postmaster would have told him who was sending Papa letters, do you?"

Once again, Elizabeth appeared upset. Abby couldn't quite put her finger on it, but she had the distinct feeling that there was something more here than the widow was letting on. "Are you alright?" she asked. "You don't look well."

"I'm fine," Elizabeth said. "Just a touch of..."

There was a knock at the door.

Abby knew at once that something was wrong. Townsfolk never came out this way after dark, and strangers on the road were always bad news. "Don't open it," she said as Elizabeth began to rise.

The widow looked at Abby, sighed, and then forced a smile onto her face. "I'm sure it's fine," she said. "It's not like we can blow out the lights and pretend that we're not here."

That was exactly what Abby wanted to do. She knew in her heart that once Elizabeth opened that door, something terrible was going to be waiting on the other side. She braced herself, thinking that someone was coming to tell her that her father was dead. She was amazed when Elizabeth opened the door and Frank Avery was standing on the front porch, grinning like the hero in a stage play.

"Ma'am," he said, "may I come in."

The widow looked him up and down, her eyes lingering on the gun belt at his waist. "I don't think that's a good idea," she said. "What seems to be the trouble."

"No trouble," he said warmly, "I just thought I'd pay Miss Abby here a visit."

"After dark?" Elizabeth said. "I don't think so."

The expression on Frank's face changed suddenly, from pleasant to deadly, and any attraction Abby had felt for the young man vanished in that moment. "Your name is Elizabeth McLarty," he said. "Your husband died two years ago when his horse kicked him in the head. What a shame, you are a beautiful woman."

The widow gasped and tried to slam the door in Frank's face, but he blocked it with his forearm. The blow must have hurt, but Avery didn't flinch. He shoved into the house, talking all the while as if he were having a leisurely conversation over tea.

"You've been in mourning ever since," he said, "but there's rumors running round that you're bedding down with Joshua Webb of the *Paradise Ledger*. So tell me, are the rumors true?"

"Abby, run!" Elizabeth shouted as Avery grabbed her from behind. His hand closed over her mouth as the widow began to scream.

The sound of her caretaker's scream jolted Abby into action. She leapt to her feet and headed not toward the back door, but to the shotgun her Papa kept leaning against the fireplace. He kept it for killing coons and coyotes and other predators that troubled their livestock. Abby knew from experience that the weapon was loaded, and if she could just lay her hands on it, she might have a chance of fending off the predator that had come in her home. She grabbed the shotgun, hefted it to her shoulder, and leveled it at Avery and Elizabeth.

"Let her go," said Abby.

Avery grinned. "If you shoot me, you'll shoot her as well," he said.

"You don't know that."

"A shotgun at this close of range... I'm pretty sure you'd kill us both," he said.

"Let her go," Abby said again.

"I don't think so. In fact, I'm going to have to ask you to drop that gun and come with me."

"Never," said Abby. "What do you want with us anyway?"

"It's not you," said Avery, "you seem like a nice kid. It's your father we want."

"What about my father?"

"He's caused some trouble for some people I work for. Stuck his nose where it didn't belong."

"I thought you said you worked for Mr. Farnum," said Abby. "Is he part of this?"

Frank smiled. "Why don't you just put down that gun? You don't have it in you to shoot me, and we both know it. You're no killer."

"Not yet," Abby said.

"Big words for a little girl," said Avery. "But it's just a lot of talk." He drew one of his guns from its holster and pressed it against Elizabeth's temple.

"I'll tell you what," he said. "I was sent for you, Abby, and Miss McLarty here is just a bonus, if you know what I mean. She's a fine woman, and I would enjoy her, but I don't want to stand here all night, so this is what I'm going to do. You have until the count of three to drop that gun and come with me peaceably. If you don't, I'm going to blow this lovely woman's brains all over the house."

"And then I'll kill you," said Abby.

"Maybe, but there's an equal chance I can shoot you before you pull the trigger. But truth be told, I'd much rather not kill anyone tonight. This is my best suit. Anyway, One..."

Abby looked from Frank to Elizabeth. She was terrified, expecting death to swoop down on her at any moment. It was up to her, Abby realized. Life or death, the choice was hers."

"Two…"

Abby dropped the shotgun. "I'll go with you," she said. "But please, don't hurt us."

Avery grinned. "That's a good girl," he said. "Come on, we have a long way to go."

Abby followed the stranger into the night, knowing all the while that her life as she knew it was over. Whatever was about to happen to her, whatever they were going to do to her father, this life was done. She climbed into the back of Avery's buckboard and made no effort to struggle as he bound her hands behind her and tied a gag over her mouth. He did the same to Elizabeth, and when Abby caught a look at the woman's face, she saw tears streaming from her eyes. She knows, Abby thought. She knows that this is the end. Abby closed her eyes and prayed. Her thoughts traveled upward through the darkness, into the thousand, thousand stars twinkling overhead.

If God was up there listening, He gave no sign.

★ ★ ★ CHAPTER 5 ★ ★ ★
IF THY RIGHT HAND OFFEND THEE

The old woman's hands were clammy and the boy nearly recoiled when she began tracing the lines on his palm. He was a handsome lad, with curly black hair and hazel eyes that would capture many a woman's heart in years to come. They sat in the gypsy's tent on the grounds of the Milton Boarding School in Sparks, Maryland. The old woman, the crone, was dressed all in black and wore a knitted shawl thrown over her shoulders. Her long, white hair, scraggly as a horse's tail, fell over her shoulders and down her back. The boy sat on a short stool, his hand extended, palm up, and resting on an overturned crate. His name was John Wilkes Booth.

The crone shook her head slowly, and the boy knew at once that something was wrong. "What is it?" he asked.

Her gaze moved from his hand to his face, and Wilkes saw something terrible in her eyes. "You gonna break hearts," said the crone, "but they won't mean nothing to you."

Wilkes started to speak, but the old woman cut him off.

"You gonna die a young man, and lots a folks is gonna weep 'cos of you." She lowered her eyes and continued speaking. "I ain't never seen a worse hand, Boy, and I wish to God I hadn't see this one."

Wilkes snatched his hand away, as if the gypsy were a rabid coon instead of a crazy old woman with yellow teeth and hair on her chin. "It doesn't matter," he said. "You're a liar and a charlatan."

"No," said the crone. She looked up and their eyes met one more time. There was something there, something young Wilkes could not deny. But whatever it was, he couldn't say.

"What is it?" Wilkes demanded.

"Keep your money," said the crone. "Get out of here."

"You have to tell me." He reached for the woman's wrist, but she slithered away from him as if his hand were a serpent.

"No," she said. "Get out. Get out!"

The boy fled the gypsy's tent, but her words and the look in her eyes never left him. He slipped into the night, just as he would do fourteen years later, on the evening when he murdered the President of the United States.

"I've heard that story before," said Joshua Webb. "Sounds to me like something out of a dime novel."

"He told me about the fortune-teller while we trained under the all-seeing eye of the Society of the Cincinnati," said Boston Corbett.

They were on a train headed west across the open countryside of Kansas as Topeka, and hopefully the troubles they had found there, receded in the distance. They spent most of the previous night hiding in an old barn on the outskirts of the city. The Army pursued them into the darkness, but luck, or God, was on their side, at least for today.

They put that time to good use. Webb had worn a beard when he entered the Topeka State Hospital the day before, and now his face was clean. Corbett, who looked like a bedraggled Jesus Christ when Webb found him, appeared almost presentable now with short hair and a neatly trimmed mustache. Someone that knew him well would certainly be able to recognize the man, but all they had to do was get from the barn to the train depot. Just a few hundred yards and they would be onboard a locomotive and headed back to Colorado.

The plan, though improvised, went off without a hitch and now they were chugging across the continent. Webb's ride eastward had been meandering and long, with stops in every town along the way. This time, the train had a direct route back to Paradise. If their luck held out, Webb would be back home that night. They had a private compartment and spent the hours talking. They talked of lost loves and lost faith. They talked of family, but mostly they talked about the winding path that led Corbett to the Topeka State Hospital.

"The fear of impending doom loomed over Wilkes," Corbett said. "He was prone to fits of melancholy, did you know that? Probably what made him such a wonderful tragedian."

"It's his final role that I'm concerned with," said Webb. "I want to know more about this Society."

Corbett stared out the window at the passing landscape, his gaunt face reflected in the window as the prairie rolled on and on, the tall grass rippling in the breeze. "He took to the Society's training. He was the perfect assassin… a killer hiding in plain sight."

"Was it difficult?" Webb asked. "Your conditioning?"

Something terrible flashed in Corbett's eyes for just a moment and then it was gone. "They whipped us like niggers," he said. "The first time I met Wilkes, he was standing naked in a barn stall with his hands tied to a beam. His back was cut up something terrible, and…"

"Stop your crying," said the man in black. "Your tears are weakness, and weakness makes me sick." He drew back his whip and gave the young man another lash. Wilkes clenched his teeth, trying to endure the pain.

The man in black wore long, flowing robes and a pointed hood over his face. Only his eyes were visible, but Thomas Corbett saw nothing but death in those eyes. This man of darkness was like a demon or a god.

He stared at Corbett, taking his full measure. "Take off your clothes," he said. "Your turn is coming."

"What is it?" said Webb.

"They did things to us," Corbett said. "Terrible things. And the things they made us do... those were even worse."

"Why? For what purpose?"

Corbett smiled bitterly. "To turn us into monsters," he said. "To break us until we took pleasure in cruelty."

"My name is Wilkes," said the man with hazel eyes.

"I'm Thomas," said Corbett.

They shook hands as they sat side by side in a bare room with only a single canopy bed in the middle of the floor. Corbett felt strange as he looked at that bed, wondering if he would have to share it with this stranger. After the beating he had endured, he wanted nothing more than to collapse into dreamless sleep, but somehow, he doubted that was going to happen. Even under normal circumstances, Corbett hardly slept at night. When he lay in bed, that was when Susan's ghost came to him.

The look on her face as she realized she was never going to hold their baby—he saw that look every time he closed his eyes.

"How long have you been here?" Corbett asked.

"A few weeks?" said Wilkes. "I don't know. I've lost track of the time."

"What happens now?"

"First pain," said Wilkes, "and then pleasure."

Corbett stared at the young man without understanding.

"Just wait. You'll see."

Thomas Corbett understood when they brought the whore to them. She was a tiny thing, pale and frightened, but willing to do whatever was required of her so long as her price was met. She looked a little like Sarah, Corbett thought. Just a little bit.

Before that long night was over, that wretched whore begged them to stop. Her screams filled the house, but no one could hear her. No one that was willing to help her, in any case.

Corbett shook away the painful memories he had been revisiting. He closed his eyes, and when he opened them again, the darknessWebb had seen a moment before was gone.

"My God," said Webb. "That's terrible."

"I know," said Corbett. "I hated myself. I felt so unclean. I was a monster, and I hated the things they made me do..." He began to weep, but quickly stifled his tears.

Webb considered his traveling companion, the man for whom he had risked so much. Had freeing Boston Corbett been a terrible mistake? He was clearly mad, and now he had made him an accessory to murder. What secret, no matter how dark, could be worth this?

"How long did they keep you there?" Webb asked after a few minutes had passed.

"I... don't... know. A few months, I think. The Society turned us loose in the summer of '58," he said. "I went to Boston, where I was born again as a disciple of Jesus Christ. I changed my name to reflect the city of my rebirth and left Thomas Corbett beneath the murky waters of my baptism."

"Upon your profession of faith in Him... and in obedience to His command... I baptize you, my brother, in

the name of the Father, the Son and the Holy Ghost. Buried in the likeness of His death, raised in the likeness of His resurrection to walk in the newness of life."

The man in white robes held Corbett under the water until his sins were washed away. He pulled this new creation from the baptismal as the other parishioners clapped self-consciously.

That was the scene, the start of Corbett's new life. But as the days turned into weeks, the weeks into months, his passion for Jesus Christ began to wane and the lusts he thought were washed away by the blood of the lamb resurfaced. He walked the streets of Beantown at night, and the whores tempted him until he thought he would go mad. Sooner or later, he was going to submit to his desires and betray not only his Susan, but his Lord as well. He could not allow that to happen.

Corbett worked days as a hatter in a little shop on Merchant's Row. No one noticed as he slipped the scissors into the pocket of his coat and carried them home one Friday afternoon. He was going to a prayer meeting that night, but he had some business to take care of first.

He sat naked on the edge of his bed, the scissors in one hand and the words of Christ on his lips.

"If thy right hand offend thee, cut it off, and cast it from thee: for it is profitable for thee that one of thy *members should perish, and not that thy whole body should be cast into hell."*

"Knowing I would eventually fall," Corbett said, "I castrated myself with a pair of scissors."

"Oh my God." Webb choked back his revulsion. He had castrated young pigs on numerous occasions–slicing open their scrotum and yanking out each testicle as the animals screamed–but the thought of Corbett doing the same thing to himself was simply horrifying.

"I see that what I've told you makes you uncomfortable," said Corbett. "But you have to understand, Mr. Webb, that I was clean at last. My sins were obsolved... the things that the Society made me do... and I never, *never* wanted to sink into that Slough of Despond again.

"What did you do? What happened next?"

Corbett shrugged. 'I cleaned myself up and went to my prayer meeting. Of course, the minister was concerned about me and insisted that I see a doctor."

They rode in silence for a time, the train moving ever westward toward Colorado. Webb had a growing sense that something was wrong back home, but whether this was irrational fear or a premonition, he could not say. Finally, after a great silence weighed between then, Corbett spoke again.

"Three years later," he said, "the war began and I enlisted."

Webb nodded, thinking of his own experience with the Army in more recent years. "Where did you see action?"

"I fought at Harpers Ferry," Corbett said. "I was captured by Mosby, the Gray Ghost, and I was imprisoned at Andersonville."

"Good Lord," said Webb. "The stories about that place..."

"It was a living nightmare," Corbett said. "But in time, I was free. I rejoined the Army, but by then the war was all but over. Lee had surrendered, though there was talk that he might be playing possum. When Lincoln was murdered, those stories began to carry a bit more weight."

The president was dead and the nation was in mourning.

Nine days had passed when the men of the 16th New York Cavalry were dispatched to Caroline County, Virginia to capture the assassin. Before they left

Washington City, Boston Corbett visited the Foundry Church to commune with the Lord. He sat in the back of the sanctuary, his eyes closed and his head bowed in reverence. When he felt the presence behind him, Corbett thought for a moment that it was the Holy Ghost come to bless him, but he was mistaken.

"Don't turn around," said a stern voice that Corbett would have recognized anywhere. It was his master from the Society of the Cincinnati.

Corbett stared at his hands as memories of his training, of his imprisonment, washed over him.

"Your company has been chosen to capture Lincoln's assassin," said the man in black. "We have arranged this."

Corbett said nothing. There was nothing he could say.

"John Wilkes Booth cannot be permitted to live," said the man. "Your assignment is to see that he never returns to this city except in a box. Do you understand?"

"I do," said Corbett.

"And will you perform this task as ordered?"

Corbett struggled against his training, but his own lips betrayed him. "I will," he said.

"Why?"

"Because... you know what is best," he said, reciting a mantra he had learned in his training. "Because... you love... me."

"And I do," said the man in black.

"Did he say anything about President Lincoln?" Webb asked.

Corbett shook his head.

"Back in Topeka, you told me that the Society orchestrated the assassination. How do you know that they were involved?"

The man who shot John Wilkes Booth looked directly at Webb, and for just a moment, the editor could see the tribulation in his companion's eyes. "They were covering their tracks," he said. "They would never bother to reveal their plans to me. That's the kind of thing that only happens in the dime novels and the kind of plays Wilkes favored. The Society doesn't operate like that."

"Tell me about Booth, about your final encounter at the Garret Farm."

Corbett sighed deeply and turned away from Webb. He stared out the window into the darkness beyond.

"We tracked Wilkes to the Garrett Farm where he was hold up in a tobacco barn."

Years later, the Garretts would claim that they had no idea that the president had been murdered, and that the man in their barn introduced himself as James W. Boyd. In any case, Wilkes was trapped with a company of New York cavalry surrounding him. His accomplice, David Herold, had already surrendered, but Wilkes refused to give himself up.

"I'd rather die," he shouted when Lieutenant Doherty ordered him out of the barn.

"And you will," Doherty said. "Light him up."

Mr. Garrett tried to protest, but the order was given and Corbett did as he was commanded. He ignited and touched it to the dry-rotted boards of the old barn. The fire caught quickly, and within minutes the entire structure was engulfed in flames.

"Come out, Booth," Doherty shouted. "There's no escape for you."

Corbett watched through a gap in the boards on the far side of the old barn. The fire hadn't reached over this far as of yet, but in a minute or two, he wouldn't be able to hold this position. He was running out of time.

If he killed Wilkes now, he could claim that the assassin was about to fire a weapon. Secretary of War Stanton had ordered Wilkes be brought in alive, and that meant Corbett had to have a good reason to shoot the man unless he wanted to spend the rest of his life in jail.

He drew his colt revolver and took aim at a man whom he had once called friend. He pulled the trigger and sent a lead ball into the back of Wilkes' head. The presidential assassin collapsed to the ground, his spine severed.

"Who fired?" Doherty demanded. "Goddammit, who fired that shot?"

Corbett slipped his weapon back into its holster. "I did, sir," he said.

Doherty glared at Corbett, and then turned to another solider. "Go get him," he ordered. "If his body burns up, we're all as good as court martialed." He turned back to Corbett. "What in the hell were you thinking? We had orders to bring him in alive."

Corbett bowed his head. "I know, sir. But he was aiming his carbine..."

"He was doing no such thing." Doherty stepped forward. "I don't know what it is about you," he whispered, "but something ain't right. You did this on purpose. Did you think it would make you a hero?"

Corbett thought about the Society, about all of the wicked things he and Wilkes had endured during their training. "No, sir," he said.

"Give me your weapon," said the lieutenant. "I'm placing you under arrest."

Corbett handed over his pistol and stood motionless as his commanding officer placed him in irons—the very irons that would have shackled Wilkes' wrists if he had lived. The assassin's killer was lead to the front porch of the Garrett farmhouse where he waited as his friend's body was carried out of the barn. Wilkes was placed at Corbett's feet, a pool of blood slowly emptying from the wound at the back of his skull.

"My God," Doherty said when he took a moment to inspect the body. "He's still alive."

The soldiers and the Garretts watched in dismay as John Wilkes Booth slowly died right there on the front porch. He never opened his eyes and never spoke another word. Corbett prayed as he waited for Wilkes to die—prayed that Christ's blood would cover this sin as it had all of the others he had committed under the black cloak of the Society.

"All in all," Corbett said, "it took him the better part of two hours to meet his fate."

Webb nodded, considering the brutal irony of the situation. Booth died from a gunshot wound almost identical to the wound he had inflicted on Abraham Lincoln. "And then what happened?"

"There was talk that I would face court martial," said Corbett, "but Mr. Stanton dropped the charges. 'The rebel is dead,' he told the papers, 'and the patriot lives.'"

"And are you a patriot Mr. Corbett?"

He thought about it for a minute. "No," he said at last. "My first loyalty is to the Lord. This country has fallen away from Him, and even the terrible judgment of the Civil War is not enough to keep us on the right path. I am no patriot... no hero... I am a sinner, washed in the blood of the Lamb, and that is why I want to expose the Society of the Cincinnati. I don't know why I was allowed to live. I'm a liability because I know the truth. Their deeds must come to the light or this nation will stand in the judgment of the Lord forever."

Corbett's words lingered in Webb's mind as their train rolled ever westward. Paradise grew closer with each passing moment, but the editor's sense of unease was rising. This Society was powerful, if Corbett was to be believed. They had orchestrated the assassination of the president of the United States, and then, less than two weeks later, the murder of the most wanted fugitive in the nation. If their reach was so vast, might they also be able to pry into a distant town in the mountains of Colorado? The thought was chilling.

It was a long time before Joshua Webb was finally able to sleep. And when he finally drifted into the Land of Nod, his dreams were terrible.

★ ★ ★ CHAPTER 6 ★ ★ ★
PRISONERS OF WAR

It was well after dawn when Frank Avery and his hostages arrived at their destination. If this was to be their final destination, Elizabeth McLarty could not say, but she knew the place at once. A one-story shack with clapboard siding that was badly in need of repair, this old cabin belonged to a Scandinavian immigrant named Jan Anderson. Elizabeth's late husband, Charles, helped to build Anderson's barn, but that was a long time ago now. Jan left town when his crops failed three years ago and hadn't been seen in Paradise since. A year after that, Charles was kicked in the head by his horse and died in his own front yard. The Anderson place had stood vacant ever since. And Elizabeth's heart... that was vacant as well. Yes, she entertained hopes that Abby's father might offer his hand in marriage, but until there was a wedding, those hopes were as good as Confederate dollars.

Avery's buckboard pulled up outside of the little cabin and he climbed over the seat and into the back of the wagon. "I love this spring weather," he said casually as he helped Elizabeth and Abby to their feet. "Exhilarating, don't you think?"

One of the women might have answered if their mouths were not gagged.

"Come on," Avery said. "I'm hungry."

He lifted each of them gently to the ground as if he were taking them out to Sunday service. The feel of his hands on her hips made Elizabeth recoil, but there was nothing she could do. She was helpless, and she hated that feeling more than anything.

Avery motioned Elizabeth and Abby toward the house, and once they were inside, he closed the door behind them. The widow noticed at once that some-one had been occupying the house. There was a stack of newspapers on the kitchen table, and a packing crate from *Reynolds Mercantile* was discarded near the wood stove.

"I want to say a few things," he began, "and if you both will obey me, I can promise you that this unfortunate situation can be as pleasant as possible. Will you listen to what I have to say?"

He stared into Elizabeth's green eyes as he spoke, and after a moment, she slowly nodded. Next his eyes moved to Abby. They examined her like a farmer judging stock at the county fair. That look made Elizabeth feel itchy all over, but what could she do? "And what about you?" he asked. After a long pause, Abby nodded as well.

Elizabeth wanted to scream, to rake her nails across this monster's face, but how? And even if she somehow managed to attack this man, he would overpower her in seconds, and what then? She was helpless.

"I'm going to remove your gags while we talk," he said, "and so long as we understand one another, I'll remove the bindings from your hands as well. Fair enough?" He moved slowly behind each woman and removed the strips of cloth that covered their mouths.

Elizabeth took in a deep breath of air, thankful that at least this part of her ordeal was over. But her relief was only temporary, for she knew that the worst was yet to come. Avery planned to use them as collateral against Joshua Webb if and when he returned to Paradise. The young man had told them as much the night before.

"Now," said Avery, "I want to make something clear to you fine ladies." He looked from Elizabeth to Abby and his eyes froze on the girl. "I've been tasked with... entertaining the both of you until my employer's business with Mr. Webb is settled up. Personally, I have no desire to harm you fine ladies, but I am willing to do so if the need arises. Do you understand my meaning?"

Abby nodded as tears rolled down her cheeks.

"You'll torture us if we cause you any trouble?" Elizabeth asked. "What a big man you must be."

Avery's attention shifted from Abby to Elizabeth. He smiled warmly and then struck the widow across the face with the back of his hand. Elizabeth went down hard as the pain exploded in her jaw. She tried to fight back her tears, but they poured out of her like oil from a broken vessel.

"Now I didn't want to do that," Avery said, "but if we are going to cohabit for a time, you both need to understand that I am in charge. Is that clear?"

On the floor, stifling her tears, Elizabeth nodded bitterly.

"Now," said Avery, "I'm famished." He looked to Abby. "There's some eggs in a basket in the kitchen. I take mine over easy. You can make yours however you like." He took Elizabeth by the arm and hoisted her roughly to her feet. "How do you take yours?" he asked.

"I-I'm not hungry," she said.

"Suit yourself. Abby?"

The girl looked at Elizabeth, her eyes pleading for some escape. "Me neither," she said.

"That's your choice," said Avery. "Maybe skipping a meal would do you some good." His gaze lingered over Abby in a way that made Elizabeth cringe. "Now, those eggs. I'll take five."

He drew a knife from his pocket, flipped it open and quickly cut the bindings from Abby's wrists. She stood there for a moment, apparently unsure as to how she should proceed.

"Snap to it," Avery said, and Abby scrambled into the small kitchen and set to work.

As Abby cooked, Avery took the widow by the elbow and led her to the kitchen table that was once the heart of this little home. He pulled out a chair and guided the woman into her seat. Her hands were still bound before her, and they pricked her with a thousand needles because her circulation had been cut off for so long. Elizabeth recoiled whenever he touched her, and this time her captor allowed his hands to linger. Avery caressed her arms with his fingertips, tracing the shape of her under her clothes. She stiffened as his hands moved to her shoulders... her neck.

"Does this make you uncomfortable?" he whispered.

The widow did not speak. Her thoughts went to Charles. He used to touch her like this after a long day of work on their homestead. Her back used to hurt so badly, but she endured the pain because it was their work–their home. Charles would rub the soreness out of her muscles, and those touches would often lead to something else... something sacred.

Avery leaned forward, his lips brushing Elizabeth's ear. "They warned me not to touch the girl, but they said to do with you as I please." He kissed her ear lobe, and the widow wanted to die. I wish I were cold in the ground beside Charles, she thought. I wish Joshua would come crashing through that door to save me.

"Please..." Elizabeth said, "please stop."

Avery lightly touched the widow's hair with the tips of his fingers. He leaned over her, buried his nose in her locks and sniffed deeply. "Do you think about your husband or Editor Webb when I touch you?"

The widow closed her eyes, fighting back tears. She felt ashamed. She knew somewhere in her heart that she had done nothing wrong, but she couldn't help it. Avery's hands made her feel unclean.

When it seemed that the torture would go on forever, Abby appeared from the kitchen with a plate of steaming eggs. The look on her face told the whole story—she knew what was happening in here and rushed through her work so she could intervene. She was a good girl, and thankfully Avery hadn't ordered his eggs hard-boiled.

He ate like an animal that has wandered the desolate path of starvation. In less than a minute, the eggs were devoured and Avery was licking clean his plate. His behavior was shocking, and both women stared at him in disgust as he wiped the partially cooked egg yolk from his chin and the tip of his nose.

When he was finished with his breakfast, Avery set his plate on the table before him and grinned at Abby and Elizabeth. There was a thin crust of egg yolk drying in the bristles of his day's growth of beard. "Now," he said, "I hate to eat and run, but I have an appointment in town and I must be under way."

"What about us?" Elizabeth said before she had a chance to think about what she was doing. Her cheek was throbbing and her fear was quickly turning over to anger. She would have killed this monster if given the opportunity.

Avery wiped the egg residue from his face as he spoke. "Well, I'm going to tie the both of you to those chairs," he said. "I'm fairly certain you won't be able to escape, but if by some chance you do manage to wriggle your way free, I want to warn you that I have a confederate outside watching the house."

Elizabeth's eyes narrowed. There had been no indication of another conspirator before now, and it was possible that Avery was lying. On the other hand, the widow had every reason to believe that he was working for Jeremy Farnum, he'd told Abby as much when he came around the other day, and if that was the case he could afford to put a dozen men out there in the woods. She didn't know what to think.

"Believe me or not," Avery said, "I can see that you have your doubts, But it doesn't matter. Abby here is going to remain in my custody until this unfortunate situation is resolved. And you..."

"What about me?"

Avery smiled. "That's entirely up to you, Miss McLarty."

A grim silence filled the little house.

"Well, I have to be under way. Shall we?" He stood up and indicated that Abby should sit down in his chair. She obeyed because there was nothing else she could do.

Abby sank into the chair, weeping as Avery retrieved a rope from the far side of the room and tied her down. Then he took another chord and bound Elizabeth where she sat. When he was done, he surveyed his work like a man who has just finished splitting a large pile of firewood for the coming winter. He was pleased with himself, the widow could see it on his face as plain as day.

"My hands," she said after a panicked moment. "Are you going to leave me like this all day?" Her hands were numb from lack of circulation and she dreaded the feeling of her fingers coming back to life. Still, to leave her bound at the wrists was just torture.

The look on Avery's face reminded Elizabeth of a certain cat she once knew. He was a cruel creature that enjoyed tormenting small birds and mice–playing with them until they died. She supposed that was the way of cats, and perhaps some men as well. If Avery weren't pressed for time, he might have drawn this out for hours, but as he said, he had to go.

"That depends," he said. "Will you make me regret it if I free your hands?"

She stared at him in contempt. "No," she said.

"Do you promise?"

Elizabeth gritted her teeth. "I promise."

Avery unfolded his knife and loosed her bindings. The blood rushed into her hands, sending needles of agony into her fingers.

"I wish I didn't have to run off like this," Avery said, "but I'll see you both tonight." He tipped his hat and moseyed out of the house. A minute later, they heard hoof beats thundering away. They were alone.

They hoped.

"Do you really think he has someone out there in the woods? Abby asked.

"I don't know," said the widow. "It doesn't matter."

"I'm so sorry that he hit you... what do you mean it doesn't matter?"

"We can't stay here and do nothing. That man is a demon."

Abby tried not to stare at the bruise swelling on the widow's cheek, but it was impossible not to look. Witnessing Avery's cruelty had put a fear into the girl that she thought she might never be able to over-come. The casualness with which he struck out... he was capable of anything. And even worse, Abby had seen the way he looked at Elizabeth. If they were still here when he got back, he was going to do more than hit her friend. Abby didn't even want to think about that.

"We have to find a way out of here," Elizabeth said. She struggled against her bindings, but it was no use. The ropes wouldn't budge.

Abby closed her eyes and said a little prayer. She wanted to be free—wanted more than anything to throw off these binding and escape into the wilder-ness, but she was frightened. Did she dare? After a moment's hesitation, she realized that she had no other option. She had to try.

"Elizabeth," she said, "I have a knife."

"What?"

"I took it from the kitchen," Abby said, "when I was making the eggs. It was just lying there and…"

"…and that bastard wasn't watching you." The widow smiled ruefully. "Show me."

Abby struggled to reach the pocket on the front of her dress where she had stashed the knife while Avery was busy tormenting Elizabeth. It took some unconventional bending, but she managed to pull the small blade free. It was rusty and dull, but it was the only chance either one of them had for escape. It had to work.

Straining against her ropes, Abby managed to position the knife so the handle was in her right hand and the blade tucked beneath the chords that bound her to the chair. She began to saw. Each movement strained her muscles in ways they weren't used to being worked, but she kept at it. She paused after several minutes to relax the unfamiliar strain on her wrist.

"Do you have any idea what this is all about?" Abby asked. She had been phrasing and rephrasing this question in her mind for hours, biding her time until she had a chance to be alone with her friend. Her father was clearly in some kind of trouble, but whatever secret he had stumbled upon, this wasn't like his other stories. Ghosts and ghouls and Indian magic... you could chalk all of that stuff up to make-believe if you really wanted to. You could explain it. But this was different. No matter what happened now, no matter how this turned out, Abby knew one thing—her life would never be the same.

The widow took a deep breath before giving her answer. Whatever she knew, it wasn't good. "Your father has been receiving letters from a man in a lunatic asylum in Kansas," she said at last. "He claims to be the man who shot John Wilkes Booth."

"What? Why would he want to talk to my father?"

"I don't rightly know," said Elizabeth.

Abby knew, or at least she suspected. Her father had gained a certain reputation thanks to his work on the *Paradise Ledger*, and had become a beacon for lunatics all over the country in the years since he founded his newspaper. Each one wanted his moment in the sun, and more often than not, her father indulged them.

"The letter claimed that there was more to the conspiracy to kill President Lincoln than is commonly known," Elizabeth said. "Corbett, his name is Boston Corbett, wanted your father to talk to him at the asylum in Topeka. Said he would make everything clear."

"Lincoln... Corbett... Booth... this doesn't make any sense. And why is Mr. Farnum involved?"

"I don't know," said the widow, "but it can't be good. We need to get out of here, so get back to work on those ropes."

Abby did as she was instructed, twisting herself around the knife and sawing until her bindings finally gave way. She was free.

"Good girl!' Elizabeth said as Abby leapt to her feet and set to work on her ropes. In a few minutes, they would be able to escape this place and go get help.

Abby sawed at the widow's bindings until the ropes finally gave way. A look of powerful relief washed over Elizabeth's face, and she threw her arms around Abby, pulling her close. "Oh thank God," she whispered. "Thank God."

The girl embraced the older woman, and for just a moment she felt safe. Maybe, just maybe, everything was going to be fine. They were free, and they could run and hide somewhere where Frank Avery and Jeremy Farnum would never find them. They would warn Abby's father, and... and...

The hope fled out of Abby all at once. Her stomach twisted in a knot, and she thought for a moment that she was going to be sick. Avery warned them that he had a man out there, watching the house. If they walked out the front door, he was likely to shoot Elizabeth and recapture Abby within a few minutes. And if, by some miracle, they managed to sneak past this co-conspirator, they were miles and miles away from town. And who was there in Paradise that would be willing to help them? No one was brave enough to take a stand against Jeremy Farnum. The sheriff was Farnum's pawn, and most of the men in town either worked for him or hated her father or both.

"We can't go out there," Abby said. "What if..."

"We have to," said Elizabeth.

'But..."

"There's no choice. We can't stay here so we have to go."

"I'm afraid," Abby said. She bowed her head and tried to fight back the tears. They came anyway.

"I am too, but right now, you have to swallow your fear. Avery can't hurt you, and I don't think there's anyone watching this house."

"You don't?"

"If there were, we would have seen this confederate by now. He would have been in the house when we arrived or come to check on us when Avery went away. He's not out there leaning against a tree with a rifle trained on the house."

"How can you be sure?"

"I can't."

"But you're willing to walk out that door and risk your life?" Abby asked. The widow's confidence was giving her strength, and she needed every little bit of strength she could get right now.

"We can't stay here," Elizabeth said, "so yes I am."

Their eyes met, and both women rose as one. Elizabeth was the first to the door. She opened it slowly, took a quick look outside, and then flung it open wide. No gunshot rang out in the woods on the hill. No one said a word as Elizabeth and then Abby filed out of the old Anderson homestead and into the countryside. They headed south, back toward town. Abby felt strange walking across the open field, but once they reached the safety of the woods, her nerves eased up a little bit. They stayed off the road, knowing that this would slow their pace but deciding that it was safer to avoid contact with other travelers. Perhaps, if they were lucky, they would be able to reach Paradise by suppertime.

MARTELS

CHAPTER 7

THE PARADISE THEATER

"I think about Lincoln sometimes," Webb said. "About that speech he gave before he died."

"The one at Gettysburg?" Corbett asked.

"No. The other one. The one he gave upon his second inauguration."

"What about it?"

Webb reached into his pocket and produced a slender notebook. This was all that remained of the research he had done on his eastbound trip from Colorado to Topeka. The books he checked out of the Paradise Library—they were still stashed in his hotel room in Topeka. He didn't want to think about the cost of replacing those books. What could he do?

The editor flipped through the pages in his notebook until he came to the notes he had taken about Lincoln. "Here it is," he said. He cleared his throat and began to read:

"Fondly do we hope, fervently do we pray, that this mighty scourge of war may speedily pass away. Yet, if God wills that it continue until all the wealth piled by the bondsman's two hundred and fifty years of unrequited toil shall be sunk, and until every drop of blood drawn with the lash shall be paid by another drawn with the sword, as was said three thousand years ago, so still it must be said the judgments of the Lord are true and righteous altogether."

"Fine words," Corbett said, "and true. The Lord's judgment is coming on this guilty land, it's only a matter of when."

They rode in silence as the specter of judgment hung over them. Slavery was dead, but for Webb, the sins of his nation were legion. He himself had participated in one such abomination, when he killed women and children on the banks of the Washita River. They were casualties of war, so said General Custer, but Webb knew the truth. It was murder, and nothing he could say or do would ever change that fact in his heart. It didn't matter that he was following orders. It didn't matter that he was one among many that day, his hands would never be clean and that was a fact. When he left the Army, Webb made a vow to never again take up arms against another human being.

And perhaps the Lord could still make use of him in some way. Did he even believe that was possible? He had his doubts about Jesus Christ and the virgin birth and all of that, but here he was, on a train in Colorado instead of locked up in a jail back in Topeka. Perhaps the Lord, if he was up there, had answered his prayer. Perhaps everything was going to work out fine.

The woods would have been almost pleasant under other circumstances. Sure, there was wildlife out here in the woods of Colorado, but if Joshua were here, if they were, perhaps, sharing a picnic in that last clearing, Elizabeth would have been content in her soul. Instead, she and Abby were marching for their very lives. Every step brought them closer to town and closer to someone that might be able to help them—or turn them over to Jeremy Farnum.

"We could ask Mr. Anders," Abby said, continuing the hours-long conversation that had been going on ever since they fled the Anderson homestead.

"The trapper?"

"Papa said that he had some trouble with Mr. Farnum a few years back."

Elizabeth nodded. A number of folks had some sort of issue with the richest man in town, but would they take a stand against him... that was the question. "Something about trespassing... I don't rightly recall."

"Do you think he would help us?"

"I don't know," said the widow. "How many prospects have we got now?"

Abby thought about it for a moment, adding up the very short list of prospective heroes in her head as she walked. "Six," she said at last. "But I'm still not so sure about Mr. Reynolds."

"Your father has always spoken very highly..." Elizabeth's words trailed off as she heard the thunder of hooves in the distance. She froze in place, as did Abby, until the sound stopped. The widow doubted very much that a rider would be able to hear them this deep in the woods, but she didn't want to take any chances. She could still feel the places where

Avery's hands had touched her. She wanted to sink into a hot bath and scrub herself until her skin was raw. That man was a demon, there was no doubt about that in her mind.

"We should keep moving," Abby said when a comfortable amount of time had passed.

They had been traveling for hours, but neither woman had any idea how much time had actually passed. They were in trouble, and if they didn't get help, they would find themselves in the woods at night, and that was almost as dangerous as if they had just stayed back at the cabin.

Almost.

They began walking again, but neither spoke. Somehow, deep down, they both knew that danger was near. Elizabeth couldn't quite put her finger on it, but her heart was fluttering and she had this sickening sense that something terrible was about to happen. This was just like the day that Charles died. All that morning she felt like something was wrong, but she pushed the feelings away. And then she heard the sound of that cursed beast's hoof striking the side of her husband's head. She had that same feeling again, or something akin to it. There was perhaps nothing so terrible in this world as losing the man she loved. A part of her died that day. But here she was, wanting to live and it didn't help to compare this and that. She had to protect Abby and there was only one way to do that. They had to get to town.

The sound of hooves echoed through the woods once again, but this time it was closer. It was almost upon them. The widow froze as Abby, a few paces in front of her, turned back in horror. They both understood at once what had happened–a rider on the road heard them talking and stopped to listen.

"I think we're safe," Abby began, when Frank Avery came charging through the thicket on a huge black horse. The creature's fervent eyes were shining with terror at the man astride her back. Avery had a frantic look on his own face, likely from hours of searching for his missing hostages. Who knew what terrible penalty Jeremy Farnum might have inflicted upon his man if he lost their quarry.

"Stop!" Avery shouted as he tugged hard on the reigns. The mare reared up, but the man in the cheap suit managed to hang on to her back.

"Run!" Elizabeth shouted at the same moment. She thrust herself forward, practically pushing Abby to get moving.

It was no easy feat to run through the trees, especially in dresses, but their steps were fueled by fear. They had only the slightest hope of escaping Avery, but perhaps the Lord would intervene on their behalf and a bear might tear their pursuer to shreds. In any case, they ran because it was the only thing they could do. Unfortunately for Elizabeth, she came down awkwardly on her left foot and felt her ankle give out beneath her. She screamed as she went down, the pain exploding inside of her.

Abby stopped, and for just a moment it appeared that she was going to turn back to help her friend. No matter what happened, Elizabeth didn't want her anywhere near this monster. "Go Abby!" she shouted. "Don't worry about me, just go." She waved the girl away.

After a moment's hesitation, Abby darted into the woods like a frightened animal. She was gone, and just like that, Elizabeth knew that her life was over. She bowed her head as Avery, now dismounted, stopped in front of her. He was grinning like a lunatic and taking deep, gasping lungfuls of air.

"You shouldn't... have run," he gasped. "Wasn't... nice."

The widow glared at him, her eyes burning with hatred. "She's gone, you bastard. And I don't think you're going to be able to catch her."

Avery sighed heavily. "I'm afraid you're right," he said. "But I think you will."

"What do you mean by that?"

Avery reached for the pistol on his hip. He drew the weapon and pulled back the hammer.

A gunshot rang through the woods.

Abby knew that she should keep running, but try as she might, she couldn't will her feet to move.

"Abby," came a cracking voice through the trees. It was Avery. "Abby, I know you can hear me."

She stood perfectly still, pressing her small body against the trunk of a tree. If she didn't move an inch, maybe whatever terrible fate this evil man had waiting for her would pass her by.

"Abby," Avery shouted, "you might be able to escape, but if you do, know this. I'm going to rape your friend here. And when I'm done, I'm going to put a bullet in her forehead like a hog."

Abby felt hot tears spill from her eyes. Run, she told herself. Elizabeth told you to run and so you should run. But her legs simply would not obey.

"The widow here is awfully pretty Abby. It's a shame what's going to happen to her. But you could stop it if you come on back right now."

"Don't do it Abby," Elizabeth shouted. "Ru…"

There was a sound like splitting firewood. Abby didn't want to imagine what could have made that sound, but she imagined it anyway. She pictured Avery bringing the butt of his pistol down on the back of Elizabeth's head. The man was a demon and he was using Abby's goodness as a weapon against her. What kind of a friend would she be to Elizabeth if she left her there?

"She's bleeding pretty bad now Abby," Avery said. "If you're going to run, I might as well get started here."

"Wait!" Abby whispered. She knew that she shouldn't say a word, that she should flee while she still had the chance, but she couldn't help herself. "Wait," she said again, louder this time. "I'm coming."

Finally her legs started working again, but they were carrying her in the wrong direction. Paradise was to the south, but here she was, heading back to the man that had taken her away from her home. There were a handful of people in town that might be able to help her–five or six that she and Elizabeth had named as potential allies–but they were all hours away in the other direction. She tromped through the undergrowth, snagging the hem of her dress on wild blackberry vines, but Abby paid no attention to that. All that mattered was Elizabeth. How could she ever forgive herself if something happened to her friend and she did nothing? No, this nightmare had to end and it had to end here and now. She wasn't sure of how she was going to do it, but Abby meant to kill Frank Avery.

I should have done it back at the house when I had the chance, she thought. She didn't think she had it in her, but she knew without a doubt that if she had the opportunity again, she would pull the trigger on this monster without a moment's hesitation. Even if it meant her own life was sacrificed as well.

Abby's heart broke when she reached the spot where Elizabeth fell. There was her friend, lying face down in last year's leaves. Her black dress and her hair were wet with blood and she wasn't moving.

Avery stood over her, twirling his pistol around his finger like a sharpshooter in one of those traveling Wild West shows. He smiled when Abby came into sight, and the thought that that grin once set her heart to fluttering made the girl want to vomit. *How could I have been such a fool?*

"Welcome back young Miss Webb. I'm pleased to see that you took my threat seriously. I knew that a good hearted young woman such as yourself..."

Abby strode across the tiny distance between them and, without warning, struck Avery across the face with every ounce of hatred in her soul. The man's entire body turned with the blow. His finger, still in the trigger guard of his pistol, tightened involuntarily and a second shot rang out in the woods. Abby drew back her fist to strike him again, but Avery had recovered his wits by that time and he caught her by the wrist in mid-strike.

Acting purely on instinct, Avery used Abby's momentum against her. He flung her violently to the ground. Abby landed in a heap as her breath was knocked from her lungs. She gasped for air as dirt and leaves filled her mouth. Avery was on her back a moment later, and she thought that he was about to take her by force. She closed her eyes, preparing for the worst as Avery began to touch her all over.

"Pretty little wench like you," he whispered into her ear, "I could have a lot of fun with you."

"Burn in hell," Abby said through clenched teeth.

"I probably will, " Avery said, "but that's not my concern right this minute. Right now, I have to take you to see Mr. Farnum."

"I won't go," Abby said. "You'll have to drag me."

"I will do it if it comes to that," Avery said. "But it would certainly be easier if you just walked beside me like a good girl."

"What about Elizabeth?" Abby asked. "Is she..."

"Dead?" Avery asked. He shook his head. "Gonna have a hell of a headache when she wakens up, but you don't need to concern yourself..."

"I'm not going anywhere without her," Abby said. "I mean that you bastard."

"Such language. Does your father know you talk like that?"

Abby spat in his face. Avery drew back for a moment, his hand quivering as if it were about to strike, but he quickly regained his composure. "Don't do that again," he warned.

"Will you hit me next time?" Abby asked.

"I might. And that would be bad for both of us," Avery said. "Now, if you will assist me, we can walk Miss McLarty back to the road and be on our way. Is that agreeable?"

Abby stared at him with pure hatred in her eyes. Only minutes ago she was free, and now here she was again, a prisoner of this demon. Perhaps she should have kept running, but she would have never been able to live with herself leaving Elizabeth behind like that. No, she did what she had to do. No matter what happened next, at least she could rest in the knowledge that she stood by her friend.

Avery climbed off of Abby and then extended his hand to help her up. She almost reached for it, but then thought better of it. She flipped over onto her side and then slithered to her feet. I would rather crawl than accept help from *him*, she thought.

"Tend to your friend," Avery said. "But be quick about it. Mr. Farnum wants to see you right away."

Abby went to Elizabeth, who hadn't moved an inch in the minutes since Abby arrived on the scene. The girl knelt over her friend, smoothing back her hair so she could get a better look at her wound. The widow was bleeding badly from the back of her head and she had a swollen lump there that pained Abby to even look upon. But she was breathing, and that was something.

"Elizabeth?" Abby said.

She said nothing.

"Can you hear me?"

The widow groaned.

"Listen," said Abby, "I know that you said I should run, but I just couldn't leave you with him. I'm sorry."

Elizabeth finally stirred. Her voice was weak and each word was an agony, but Abby listened intently, not wanting to miss a word. "Y-you... should... have run," she whispered.

"You're welcome," Abby said, choking back her tears. How had her life dissolved into this nightmare in such a short space of time? All of this seemed like a nightmare, and that at any moment she might awaken in the darkness of her room with her father sitting at the foot of her bed. She wanted that more than anything—for life to go back to the way it was before that cursed letter changed everything. But alas, this was no dream. This nightmare was real, and if she didn't find a way out of it, both she and Elizabeth were in serious trouble.

"Th-thank you," Elizabeth said after a long moment. She struggled to her knees and would have fallen without Abby's help.

"We're going to get out of this," Abby said. "Do you hear me?"

Elizabeth smiled wanly. "I hear you," she said. "I don't know if I can believe it, but..."

"Believe it," said Abby, standing. She extended her hand and Elizabeth took it.

"Come on now," Avery said. "We have an appointment with Mr. Farnum and we don't want to be any later than we already are. He motioned toward the road and the two women began to walk. He followed behind them, leading his horse by the reins. It was getting dark.

When the train arrived in Paradise that evening, two shabbily dressed men stepped out onto the platform. One might have seemed familiar to the townsfolk, though few had seen the man clean-shaven. He was the madman, the lunatic editor of a newspaper that brought shame upon the community. There wasn't a man in town that called him friend. The other man's name was infamous throughout the nation, but his face was not so well known. He was the assassin's assassin, the man who shot John Wilkes Booth, but his name he left behind in Topeka. He was running, and that name was an albatross around his neck.

"Memories of the Society have begun to surface in my mind, in the years since," said Corbett.

"Shhh!"

"Sorry," Corbett whispered. "Sometimes I don't think straight."

Webb motioned for his companion to head down the platform stairs. The editor moved with the deliberate ease of someone that had walked those steps hundreds of times, but Corbett was different. Each step was that of a frail old man afraid that it might be his last. Whatever torments he had endured during his time in the sanitarium, not to mention those in the years leading up to his incarceration, had taken their toll on the man. At least the wound in his shoulder seemed to be giving him little trouble.

"Where are we headed now?" Corbett asked once they reached the safety of the ground.

"We have to get you to a secure location," said Webb. "Some place they'll never think to look for you."

"What do you have in mind?"

Webb's eyes went from Corbett to a building at the far end of the street. It was lit up with red-tinted lanterns that practically made the structure glow in the deepening darkness of the evening. The sign was plainly readable, even from this distance. *The Paradise Theater* was painted in huge letters on the side of the building.

"The theater?" Corbett asked.

"Calling that place a theater is a joke," said Webb. "It's a whorehouse, plain and simple, but this is the last place anyone who knows your peculiar history would ever look for you."

"Are you sure about this?"

"No," said Webb. "But I'm not sure about anything right now, and until I get my thoughts straight, I think keeping you hidden is the best course of action."

Corbett shrugged. "Very well," he said. "Fallen women hold no sway over me."

"I suppose they don't. In any case, I don't have any better ideas at the moment." Webb led the way and the two men headed toward the brothel.

★ ★ ★ CHAPTER 8 ★ ★ ★
THE MAN IN WHITE

He laid a towel over the chair so as not to soil the seat of his trousers. The old Anderson house was in shambles and, other than Frank Avery, hadn't been lived in by anything other than coons and possums in three years. Even when Jan dwelt in the place it hadn't seen a woman's touch, for that old immigrant was either fancy or a perpetual bachelor or both. In other words, the cabin was as far from the conditions to which Jeremy Farnum was accustomed that the richest man in Paradise seemed as out of place here as Reverend Cates might have in the *Paradise Theater*.

Farnum grinned amiably as he crossed his legs and surveyed the filthy room by the light of a single lantern. "Quite a place," he said. "Appalling, really."

"Imagine it... from my point of view," Elizabeth said, and Abby nearly laughed out loud at the stinging honesty of her friend's words. The widow was much improved since they had returned to the Anderson house, but there was still something not quite right about her speech. Her words came slower than normal, and she seemed to be having trouble getting them out. But that wasn't what worried Abby most. Elizabeth seemed to have given herself over to darkness. It was like she knew something terrible was coming and that there wasn't anything that she could do about it.

"I apologize for these accommodations," Farnum said, "But I'm sure you can understand that I couldn't exactly put you up at the *Paradise Hotel*."

The widow stared at him with half-vacant eyes. Her face was swollen and there was blood caked in her hair. "You could... have left us well enough alone," she said.

"I wish that were the case," said Farnum. "I really do. Unfortunately, our friend, Mr. Webb, has put us all in a rather regrettable situation."

Abby's ears perked up at the mention of her father. "What about my father?" she demanded. "Nothing he could have done would give you a right to kidnap and torture us."

Farnum smiled condescendingly. "Child," he said, "you don't understand the situation."

"Then explain it to me."

"You want that I should do something about her pretty little mouth?" Avery asked. He seemed almost eager to inflict some kind of suffering on her.

"You just lay off," Farnum said. "Let me handle this."

Avery backed off in absolute deference. Abby wondered what kind of master could command such supplication in a servant, but decided that she didn't really want to know.

"Your father has caused some trouble in Topeka," Farnum said. "A certain... organization that I'm a member of, they didn't take too kindly to his interference."

"What does that have to do with us?" Elizabeth said. "We didn't..."

"The two of you are our insurance policy," Farnum said. "Now, I apologize for the inconsiderate actions of my associate here," he nodded at Avery, "but he is young and foolish and given to cruelty."

"He's... a demon," said the widow.

"Be that as it may," said Farnum, "he is proficient at his work. I'm sure you wouldn't disagree Miss McLarty."

She stared at the man in horrible agreement, and Abby felt whatever hope she had left die in her heart. There was no way out of here–no way to escape this evil man and his minion. Whatever trouble her father had gotten himself into, it must be something terrible.

"What would your wife... say if she knew you... were keeping us here?"

A glimmer of something shadowed Farnum's face, but then it was gone. "Well, that's something I'll concern myself when it happens," he said. "But don't worry your pretty little head over it."

The widow stiffened.

"I never really noticed it before," he said, "but you are a beautiful woman, Miss McLarty. Has Mr. Webb ever told you that?" Farnum reached out and touched Elizabeth gently on her cheek. She turned her head away, but Farnum took her by the chin and forced her to look at him. "Now listen close," he said, "I want you to know that I feel very badly about this whole situation. It's most unfortunate, but alas, everything must serve the greater good. Wouldn't you agree? And in spite of the hardships that you and young Miss Webb here have endured, allow me to promise you that it *does* serve the greater good."

"How reassuring," said the widow.

"Now, since clearly Frank here hasn't been able to keep the both of you comfortable and in one place, I've decided that it's best if I take charge of Abby."

"No," Abby said before she even realized that she was speaking.

"No," Elizabeth said, at almost exactly the same moment.

Abby pictured what might happen to her friend if she were left behind with Avery. The thought made her convulse all over. She thought also what might happen to her in the custody of Jeremy Farnum. He was polite, if nothing else, and she couldn't image him striking her, which was a very real possibility with Avery. On the other hand, she could picture her father coming to this little shack and rescuing her, and if she went to the Farnum place, she doubted that she would ever leave alive.

"I'm afraid so," said Farnum. "We're leaving momentarily. I'm not taking any chances on another escape." As he spoke his eyes shifted to Avery. The young man bowed his head as if he were ashamed of displeasing his father. What was it that these two shared?

"What do you want me to do with Miss McLarty?" Avery asked.

Farnum looked from Avery to Elizabeth. Abby could tell that there was something in that look, something that meant trouble for her friend. "I have every reason to believe that Mr. Webb and his... companion... are on their way back to Paradise," he said. "They could be here as early as tonight, by my reckoning."

"You mean it's time to..."

"Yes," said Farnum. "Be about it and no more mistakes. Do you understand me?"

"Yes, sir."

Jeremy Farnum rose, and with one swift motion grabbed Abby by the arm. She tried to pull away, but his grip was like iron. He began dragging her toward the door, and only after she had taken a few shuffling steps did Abby begin to scream. Elizabeth stood up, ready to throw herself in between Abby and her abductor, but Avery wrapped his arms around the widow in a terrible embrace.

"You stay here with me," he said in a stage whisper, "we've got a lot to do, you and I."

"Eliz…" Abby cried, but Farnum silenced her with a hand over her mouth. He drug her out into the night, and within minutes she was up on the back of his horse and galloping toward town. She would have thrown herself from the horse but Farnum rode behind her, his strong arms holding her in place. Abby wept because it was the only thing she could do.

The inside of the *Paradise Theater* was just as gaudy as the exterior. Murals depicting the fall of Eve and Bathsheba bathing on the roof and naked sirens out of mythology covered the walls in sordid detail. In all his years in Paradise, Joshua had never visited this place. He might have, as a man fresh out of the army, but at first he was too busy setting up his homestead, and then, when he met Sarah, the thought of laying with another woman was anathema to him. When Sarah was gone, when sometimes the loneliness became too much for him, Webb nearly broke down and came to this place many times. But then he thought of Abby, of this disappointment that would forever cloud her eyes if she found out that he visited a whore, and he turned right around and went back to his room. Still, the editor found his eyes wandering to the scandalous paintings that covered the walls, and then drifting, as was certainly the intention of this establishment's proprietor, to the scantily clad women that sauntered around the room in search of their next conquest.

"This place is a den of corruption," said Corbett, willfully staring at his boots as if they were a painting by Leonardo DaVinci.

"I know," said Webb. "Why don't you sit down at that table over there. I'll be right back."

"Fine," Corbett said. "But don't be long." He sat down behind a circular table and almost immediately a woman with long, dark hair slithered up behind him. She leaned over him, roughly massaging his neck as she whispered into his ear.

"Hello cowboy," she said. "I don't think I've seen you around here before. I'm sure I'd remember you."

Corbett stiffened. "Get behind me, Satan."

Smiling in spite of himself, Webb headed to the bar. Luke Ashford, the owner of the *Paradise Theater*, was standing there, drying a glass with a dirty rag and eyeing the editor warily. He had bushy mutton-chops on either side of his face, perhaps to make up for the hair that was thinning on top of his head. It took him several moments before a look of strange recognition passed over his face.

"Editor Webb?"

Webb leaned over the bar, speaking in almost a whisper though there was little concern that anyone would be able to overhear him amid the din of this place. "Luke," he said, "I need your help."

No stranger to peculiar requests, Ashford leaned in close. "What is it?"

"That man over there," Webb said, "he's in trouble."

"What do you want me to do about it? I ain't getting in the way of the law.."

"Nothing like that," said Webb. "He just needs a place to hide out for a few days..."

"Did he rob the train? Or a bank? I really can't have a criminal hiding out in my place."

"No. He's harmless. A bit daft in the head, that's all. He's convinced that a secret society is out to get him."

Ashford scoffed. "Working on another one of your stories I see?"

"Something like that."

"He's not going to smash up my place or anything like that? Or summon a legion of walking dead?"

Webb wanted to come over the counter and throttle the man, but this was one instance where his reputation worked to his advantage, so he let the remark pass. What mattered now was keeping Corbett out of sight while he made sure that Abby and Elizabeth were both fine. He had a pressing need to get back home, and all that stood in his way was satisfying this man's greed. Webb removed a roll of cash from the pocket of his coat and handed the money to the bartender. "I hope this will cover his expenses," he said. "If not, I'll pay you the difference when I return."

Ashford took his time counting the money. After a few moments, he nodded solemnly at Webb. "Don't you worry," he said. "I'll take care of everything."

Webb returned to Corbett, who had dispensed with the whore by this time. He looked up at the editor with eyes that penetrated Webb to his very soul. "I've made arrangements for you," Webb said. "You're going to be staying here for a few days."

"I'd rather sleep in a ditch."

"Be that as it may, you're less likely to be spotted here."

"I will not give in to these daughters of Jezebel."

"I hate to leave you here," said Webb, "but I have to be sure that everything is fine at home."

"I pray that your daughter and your friend are well," said Corbett. Somehow, his words filled Webb with a preternatural dread. Something was wrong, he felt it, and he would not be able to rest easy until he saw that Abby and Elizabeth were safe.

Back in the Anderson house, Avery began to fondle Elizabeth the moment his master was out of sight. She tried to resist him, but he was too strong for her and whatever strength she had was fled after their encounter in the woods earlier that day. She braced herself as he ran his hands all over her and began kissing her neck as if he were Charles or even Joshua. Please, she thought, please God, let me die right here before this goes any farther. This prayer, like so many others, went unanswered.

When Avery was done, Elizabeth curled up around her own knees and waited for him to get dressed. She was cold and exposed, laying naked on the floor of this filthy cabin, but the act of dressing in front of this man–of pretending that everything was still normal and that he hadn't just forced himself upon her–somehow she couldn't bring herself to do that. If she just lay here, unmoving, maybe it would all be a dream.

"I'm sorry if I was too rough on you," Avery said. "Did I hurt you?"

Elizabeth ignored him. She thought of Charles, of the last time they made love before he was taken from her. She had not been with a man in the ensuing years, and she wondered in the depths of her mind if she had now sinned against her husband. Was he up in Heaven, watching as Avery shoved her to the floor and took her like an animal? Was he ashamed of her now? Or was Charles simply asleep in the dirt over in the town cemetery? The widow closed her eyes and wished for death.

"Now I know that this isn't going to be pleasant," Avery continued, "but I'm afraid that your friend, Mr. Webb, needs some sign of the seriousness of his situation."

Elizabeth heard him talking, but he sounded distant, like somebody speaking in another room. Part of her, whatever remained of the sensible woman that Charles had fallen in love with, that Joshua had hired as an assistant at the *Paradise Ledger*, that part knew that her torture was far from over.

Suddenly, Avery was on top of her again. Elizabeth did not resist, knowing that any struggle on her part would be futile. But this time her captor didn't force himself inside her–this time he wrestled her left arm behind her back. The widow screamed as he wrenched her shoulder out of its socket, and then she felt his fingers prodding at her face.

"Please," she gasped, but she knew her words fell on deaf ears. There was a dull pain followed by something intolerably sharp. She screamed again as darkness took her. Her last thought as she drifted away from consciousness, was this:

I hope I never wake up.

There was a lantern burning at the Webb Homestead, but when the editor reached his house he had a sense that something was amiss. He had spent years in the Army, and had grown accustomed to trusting his gut in situations where his eyes might lead him astray. Webb had wondered on his way out here if perhaps he first should have checked Elizabeth's place in town, or at the newspaper, but his heart told him that he had to go home. His horse, stabled at the livery since he left for Topeka, galloped for home as if he sensed that a few seconds might make all the difference. And now here he was, staring at his tiny house and the light burning just inside. Perhaps Abby was in there, ready to throw her arms around him the moment that he walked through the door. Perhaps Elizabeth was there as well, and if she was, he wanted more than anything to take the widow into his arms and kiss her like she was his wife. But he knew in his heart that whatever he found on the other side of that door was going to mean trouble for him and his.

The stars were twinkling overhead. He read somewhere that those stars were millions of miles away—that their light was older than the earth... that those stars might have died before Christ was born. Standing in their cold, dead light, Webb reached for the axe that was leaning against a stump in the yard. He climbed the stairs that led to the front porch, stopping at the front door. He noticed that it wasn't shut all the way. It was a bad habit of Abby's to leave the door cracked, especially in the winter, but somehow Webb knew that this wasn't his daughter's doing.

"Abby?" he said. "Elizabeth?"

No answer. The homestead was as silent as death.

He pushed open the door. *I'll never forgive myself if they've been hurt*, he thought.

He shuffled inside, stopping as soon as he crossed the threshold of the house. There was a man sitting at his kitchen table–a man he didn't know. His feet were propped up on the table, the soles of his cowboy boots caked in mud and horseshit. He had a cigar in his mouth and was leaning back in his chair with his hands laced behind his neck. A tendril of smoke rose from the end of a cigar that was tucked between his teeth, and he wore a white cowboy hat pushed back on his head. He was smiling as he looked at Webb, an expression that at once filled the editor with both fear and revulsion. There was a canvass sack sitting on the table beside the stranger's boots. It was wet with something that might have been blood, Webb couldn't tell in this light.

"Who the hell are you?" he demanded.

The stranger removed the cigar from his mouth. "Joshua Webb, I presume? My name's Frank Avery."

"What are you doing in my house? Where's Abby?"

Avery winked. "I made your daughter's acquaintance while you were away."

"Where is she?" Webb took a few paces into the room, his fingers tightening around the axe handle.

"Oh, she's safe enough for the moment," Avery said. "She's a real pretty little thing, your girl."

Webb began to draw back with the axe, ready to strike this stranger's head clean off if it came to that, but the sound of a pistol being cocked stopped him in his tracks.

"I wouldn't advise trying anything, Mr. Webb. I'm not the fastest draw in the West, but I'd wager that I'm fast enough."

The editor stared at Avery for a moment, studying the man's eyes. Many a fool had drawn on someone with no intention to pull the trigger, but Webb could see right away that this man was a killer. His axe clattered to the wooden floor. Avery leaned forward in his chair, his grin widening.

"I know that you helped Boston Corbett to escape from the Topeka State Hospital," he said. "Now, take a look inside this bag and you tell me if you think it was worth it." He nodded at the canvass sack on the table.

Webb reached for it slowly, dragging it across the table so that he could look inside. He noticed that the bag left a dribble of something behind it that could only be blood. He looked inside and suddenly had to fight the urge to vomit.

"Now, Mr. Webb, I want you to take me to wherever Corbett is hiding out. After that, we'll pay a visit to your girl and the lovely Widow McLarty. You know, some women look awfully good in black."

Webb set the sack back on the table. He was trembling all over and tears were streaming down his cheeks.

"Do you find those terms agreeable, Mr. Webb?"

"Yes," he whispered. He wiped away the tears, trying to will the image out of his mind, but he could not. He knew that it would be emblazoned there forever—a single human eye... green... just like Elizabeth's.

★ ★ ★ CHAPTER 9 ★ ★ ★
GRASPING FOR THE WIND

The nightmare flight from Webb's homestead back to the *Paradise Theater* felt like it took hours. The editor's stomach was turning over and over the entire time as he thought about Elizabeth and Abby and the horrors they must have endured at the hands of this demon. By all appearances, Frank Avery was an agent of the Society of the Cincinnati–a young operative much like Corbett and Booth back before the war. And now this organization, responsible for the murder of a president, had mutilated a woman he had come to love. And they had his girl.

They rode in silence in Avery's buckboard, bouncing along the dusky road as the lights of Paradise brightened in the distance.

I've never felt this way before, Webb thought as they pulled up outside the theater. I want to wrap my hands around this man's throat, but I can't do that. I never should have taken this story. I lost Sarah, I can't bear the thought of losing Abby as well. And Elizabeth...

"I'm a-gonna stay right here," Avery said. "But don't be too long. I'd hate to keep young Abby waiting." He smiled, and it took every bit of will that Webb could muster not to assault the man.

Swallowing his anger, Webb left Avery and headed into the *Paradise Theater*. He passed through the garish doors and into a perpetual cloud of cumulus smoke that dominated the main room of the brothel. The place was crowded, much more so than earlier in the evening, and the editor recognized quite a number of faces from town. These were men of enterprise, family men most of them, but they were somehow able to justify spending time in this den of debauchery. I've been such a fool, Webb thought as he scanned the room, looking for someone–anyone–that might be able to help him now in his hour of need. His eyes picked one brutish man out of the haze of cigar smoke. He was tall and broad, like a mountain, and instantly recognizable in a buckskin coat complete with fringe. His hair was unkempt, his beard untrimmed and streaked with silver, and Webb saw in this man his one hope of evening the odds against the Society of the Cincinnati. His name was Harris Anders. He was a trapper that dwelt in the mountain country around Paradise. He clenched a glass of beer in his hands, and he stared deeply into it as if all of the answers of life and death might be found at the bottom. He wore a tomahawk in a sheath on his belt, and his rifle was propped against the bar.

It seemed to Webb that hope was lost until he laid eyes on Anders. He was a true mountain man, full of piss and vinegar, but he was known around town as a fair man. He once helped Sarah get home when her horse threw a shoe outside of town. She said he was a perfect gentleman the entire time. Perhaps he could be persuaded to help Abby and Elizabeth.

Webb approached the bar slowly, not wanting to startle his one hope of salvation. He sat down beside Anders, but before he could speak, the bartender stepped up and asked if Webb wanted a drink.

"Not right now. Luke, can you go get the man I left here in your care?"

The bartender eyed him cautiously. "Sure thing." He moved into the crowded room and sent one of his girls upstairs to fetch Corbett.

Webb turned to Anders and whispered to him as loudly as he dared. "I'm in a world of trouble right about now," he said.

The trapper took a long swallow of his beer. "What seems to be the problem?" he never took his eyes off the glass.

"There's a man outside," said Webb. "He's taken my girl and the Widow McLarty. Says I have to turn over a friend of mine or he'll..."

"Sounds to me like you should give up your friend," said Anders.

"It's not as simple as that. And there's more. He..."

"What is it?"

"He hurt Elizabeth. Her... her eye. He... her eye was..." Try as he might, Webb couldn't bring himself to describe what had happened to Elizabeth. "Can you help me? I'll pay you anything you ask."

"I don't want your money, Webb. There ain't a man in this town that would give you a drink of water if you was dying of thirst, you know that."

"I know."

"But I like the widow and I like your girl. Reminds me of your pretty wife, she does. And I can't stand the thought of anyone hurting either one of them."

"So you'll help me?"

Anders finished his beer in one swallow. He gave out a satisfied gasp. "Yeah, I'll help you."

"Mr. Webb?" came a familiar voice. The editor turned around and saw Corbett standing there behind him.

"Boston..."

"I didn't expect to see you so soon," said Corbett. "Have you come to liberate me from these whores of Babylon?"

Webb tried for a moment to hide the fear in his face, but the effort was futile. "Boston," he said, "they've got my girl. There was a man at my house... I think he was from the Society. He said he would hurt Abby if I don't turn you over to them. I want to help you but..."

"You're correct to trust your instincts," Corbett said. "Threatening the innocent is precisely what the godless swine of the Society would do. Lead the way, I will follow you and the Lord will protect me if it is his will."

"What do you want me to do?" Anders asked. "I could follow you out right now and give that sumbitch the scare of his life."

"No," said Webb. "He's the only one that knows where I can find Abby and Elizabeth. We have to let him take us to them."

Anders nodded. "I'll follow along behind you," he said. "And when the time is right..." his words trailed off, but they all knew what he meant.

"Is there anyone else in this den of Bathsheba who might help us?" Corbett asked.

Webb took another look around the room. Time was running out. "No," he said. "Not a one."

"Then lead on," said Corbett, "and may the Lord's will be done."

They headed out of the *Paradise Theater*, down the front stairs and onto the street. Avery stood just a few empty yards away, leaning against his buckboard and puffing on a cigar. He lowered his hand to his pistol, eyeing Corbett warily. He was like a coiled snake, ready to strike at a moment's notice.

"Corbett," Avery said, grinning. Had they perhaps met at some Society proving ground in the years before the Civil War? No, Avery was too young for that.

"Gun or no gun," said Corbett, " I could leave you lying in the street, Infidel."

"Anytime you want to try me, old man," Avery said. "But you might want to think of this poor fella's little jilly out there, all alone and terrified…"

"Enough!" said Webb. "Take us to my daughter."

Avery climbed into the bed of the buckboard while Webb and Corbett got into the front seat. The younger man gave them some instructions, and the party rolled out into the night. After several minutes, Harris Anders exited the theater and pulled himself onto the back of his horse. He turned the nag in the direction that the wagon had gone, and then followed behind at a slow, steady pace.

Webb lost track of the time as they crossed the great black landscape of Colorado at night. His thoughts were ever of Abby and Elizabeth. He thought about the abomination he had seen, and in spite of himself, he found his heart and his mind turning once more to prayer. Was God up there listening? This was the same God who allowed Sarah to die… who allowed Elizabeth to be maimed and Abby to be taken hostage. The same God who allowed his own son to be sacrificed for the sins of man. Webb couldn't under-stand that, but the prayer gave him hope and so he went through the motions. He was here and not dead or jailed in Topeka, that was something.

Morning was breaking when they finally arrived at the long abandoned cabin that once belonged to Jan Anderson. Webb knew the place, though he hadn't been out this way for many years. Was Abby in there? Was Elizabeth still alive? Webb sat frozen in the front seat of the buckboard as Avery leaned forward from the bed like a child on the way home from Sunday service.

"Why don't you head on inside, Mr. Webb," he said. "Me and Boston here need to have us a little palaver."

Webb turned to the man who had done this—who had brought such trouble into his life. "I'm warning you," he said, "this isn't over by a long shot."

Avery smiled his charming smile. "No, sir," he said, "not by a long shot."

The editor climbed cautiously down from the wagon. He wanted to run the second that his boots hit the ground, but he forced himself to walk... to be calm. Whatever was waiting for him in that house, a few seconds more weren't going to matter.

He steeled his heart against whatever horror awaited him. Bracing himself, Webb opened the door.

"He's right," Avery said once Webb was out sight," This mess that you started is just beginning."

Corbett shifted uncomfortably in the wagon, his eyes never wavering as Webb approached the house, opened the door and went inside. Somewhere, deep inside of him, he felt terrible for dragging the editor into this situation. But he was trapped in the asylum, and Webb offered him a means of escape so he took it. He couldn't be blamed... couldn't blame himself really. He did what anyone would have done in a similar situation.

"What the hell were you thinking, Corbett? You durned fool."

Corbett turned back to look at Avery "Tell me, what's he going to find in there?" What have you done to his daughter?" He heard the sound of a hammer being cocked and felt the tip of Avery's revolver press into his back.

"Don't you worry your pretty head about that," Avery said. "Now get down on the ground."

Corbett complied, climbing down from the wagon and turning to face his nemesis. He kept one hand behind his back, concealing the fact that he still held the horses' reigns in that hand.

"Now tell me," Avery said, "how much have you told Webb about the Society of the Cincinnati?"

"I told him everything. He's going to expose the Society in his newspaper."

"Damn you, Corbett. You should have kept your mouth shut, but you never knew how to follow orders."

Corbett's features hardened. This fool was blathering about the mouth when he should have been focusing on the task at hand. Couldn't he see that the time for talking was over? Now was the time for blood.

"Make your move you son of serpents," Corbett said.

"Fair enough," said Avery. He pulled the trigger on his pistol and an explosion rang out through the wilderness.

At the same moment, Corbett jerked the horses' reigns, pulling them around and in front of him. He ducked down behind them as they reared up between he and his enemy. Avery's bullet grazed the closer animal's neck and blood pumped from the wound as the animal died screaming. The other horse reared a second time, neighing madly and answering her mate's death knell.

The remaining horse towered over Avery, and with one fluid motion knocked the pistol from his hand. The weapon flew from his grasp, falling to the ground and out of usefulness. As Avery staggered back, Corbett ducked out from behind the dying horse and charged at him. His fist caught the younger man square on the jaw and nearly lifting him off his feet. Corbett screamed as he made contact, for at that moment the wound in his shoulder tore open. His shirt was instantly soaked with blood.

Avery collapsed to the ground as Corbett hunkered over him. He tried to follow through, but he was already too weak. Avery recovered fast, kicking Corbett in the gut and knocking his breath away. The older man went down hard. The two men fell into a wrestling contest, as nearly all fights are apt to do, and Avery ended up on top with his fingers wrapped around Corbett's neck. There was murder in his eyes and it was plain to see that he meant to end the life of the man who shot John Wilkes Booth.

"I heard you got shot back in Kansas," Avery said as Corbett's face began to turn purple. "Looks like your wound has reopened."

Corbett struggled to free himself, but he was growing weaker by the second. There was nothing he could do. Silently, he began to make peace with God.

"You betrayed the Society, Corbett," Avery said. "Now you're gonna die."

He squeezed tighter and Corbett felt his soul beginning to drift. His strength was gone, all the fight was out of him, and he was ready to embrace death. But just as his eyes were beginning to close, he saw Avery jar suddenly and topple backward off of him. He had a sense of something zipping through the air, but he was half dead and didn't really understand what was happening.

"Is he dead?" came a muffled voice above Corbett. It took the dying man a few moments to realize that the voice belonged to Harris Anders.

"I... don't..."

"You look like Hell," Anders said. He offered his hand and Corbett took it, hardly aware of what he was doing. The trapper hoisted Corbett to his feet and together they looked down on the body of Frank Avery. The younger man was sprawled in the dirt, his shirt and sack coat stained red with blood. Some of that was Corbett's blood, he knew, but most of it was his own. There was a gaping wound in his shoulder, just above his heart. He was still breathing, but it was only a matter of time.

"Nice shot," Corbett said after a few minutes.

Anders spat in the dirt. "Come on," he said, "let's go check on Webb."

The sickness hit Webb the moment he entered the cabin. He couldn't speak, couldn't move at all. There was a stench in the room, like blood and sex and fried eggs. There were several chairs overturned and a pile of rope on the floor. There was blood splattered on the walls. There were shreds of clothing, and across the room, tied to the wood stove, was a naked women lying on her stomach.

"My God... Elizabeth?"

He ran to her, like the father in that story about the prodigal son. Kneeling down beside her, Webb put his arm around her shoulder and Elizabeth recoiled as if he were a serpent. She was alive, but just barely. Webb tried not to stare at the gaping hole where her left eye used to be. She had lost a lot of blood, much of which was dried in her hair and on her face.

"Joshua?" she whispered. "Is that... really you?"

"It's me," Webb said. "I'm here."

Elizabeth melted into his arms, weeping uncontrollably.

"Who did this to you?" Webb said.

"Farnum... his lackey. But it... was... Farnum."

Webb smoothed her hair, his own tears mingling with those of the woman he loved. To think of the suffering she had endured broke his heart, but even now his thoughts turned to his daughter. "Where's Abby?"

"Farnum... took her," said Elizabeth. "Earlier..."

"Is she..."

"She was..." her words trailed off as Webb imagined the worst.

"I'm so sorry," Webb said. "This is all my fault."

Elizabeth shook her head, and Webb could see muscles twitching inside her empty eye socket. "His fault," she said.

She pressed herself against Webb, and he held her as sobs wracked her entire body. In his heart, Webb vowed that if she survived, if they both survived this ordeal, he was going to ask this broken, beautiful women to be his wife. But for now, in the golden light of morning, the only thing to do was to hold Elizabeth as she wept against him.

"Webb?" said a voice from the far side of the cabin. It was Corbett.

The editor removed his coat and wrapped it around Elizabeth, covering her nakedness. Across the room, Corbett and Anders kept their backs turned, not wanting to add to Elizabeth's shame by looking at her in this condition.

"Who did this?" Anders asked when Webb was done with his work.

"That son of a bitch that brought us here," Webb said, "and Jeremy Farnum."

"Who?" Corbett asked.

"The richest man in town," Webb said. "And he has my girl."

"What are we gonna do?" Anders asked.

Webb's eyes narrowed. "I'm going to kill Jeremy Farnum."

CHAPTER 10

HIS SOUL GOES MARCHING ON

October 16, 1884. The narrow streets of Harpers Ferry, West Virginia were filled with a nebulous mist. It was early morning; the first beams of sunlight were still more than thirty minutes away, but already a figure was stirring on the grounds of the old Federal Armory.

A man in a rumpled suit, its color made gray by the lightless October sky, was busily setting up some photographic equipment in the old firehouse. This place was made famous twenty-five years earlier as the location where John Brown's Raiders made their historic last stand. The ensuing years had not been kind to Harpers Ferry; after the Civil War, economic depression pillaged the town in a way that not even Old Brown could have done. Businesses closed their doors forever, and citizens of that once-thriving community loaded their wagons to "go west" at the urging of Horace Greeley, a Yankee newspaperman out of New York City.

The man in the firehouse, the color of his suit shifting slowly from gray to brown as the sun rose over the Potomac, was Joshua Webb. He stole a glance at his rented wagon across the street. He didn't notice the girl staring at him from under a pile of blankets. Abby was supposed to be asleep, but the truth was that she hadn't slept well ever since her mother died, and the bumpy ride from their hotel didn't exactly make it any easier.

Abby watched as her father made a few final adjustments to his camera, an American Optical 76. He told her all about it on the train ride from Colorado. Abby was currently entertaining the idea of being a photographer when she grew up, but at eleven, she still had a lot of growing to do and she didn't want to hold herself to anything in particular. What she wanted now, more than anything, was for her father to hold her close and tell her that they were going to be all right.

Webb returned to his wagon, which was parked on the street adjacent to the old armory. The original building was in ruins, having been destroyed by Federal troops trying to prevent the arsenal from falling into enemy hands. Now all that remained were blackened walls and the ghosts that legend held still wandered these hallowed grounds. It was the siren call of these wandering spirits that drew Joshua Webb east from his little newspaper office in Paradise, Colorado. He had heard a legend that John Brown's ghost wandered the streets of Harpers Ferry, and he vehemently informed his daughter that if he could photograph the specter, he would have concrete evidence of the supernatural world that his detractors would be forced to accept.

Abby closed her eyes as her father reached the wagon. She pretended to be asleep.

"Abby," he said, giving his daughter a gentle nudge, "it's almost time."

It was hot and it stank in her prison. Abby stood at the tiny attic window that was her only source of light and looked into the world outside–a world that she could see but that was beyond her touch. She wondered if she would ever get to walk in the sunshine again or if she was going to die up here in this dusty place.

The window overlooked the Farnum estate, and though this was the only time she had ever seen it, the house and the grounds certainly lived up to her expectations. There was a lovely garden on the south side of the house–a garden teaming with vibrant flowers and crisscrossed with footpaths. It was the kind of place where a girl could spend a few hours relaxing in the shade with a good book.

Abby wiped away a tear as her thoughts went to Elizabeth... what trials had her friend endured since they were separated? Was she even still alive? And what about her father? It was his cursed newspaper that started this trouble. His precious paper that had become the most important part of his life since her mother died. He put in the minimum amount of time at home that he possibly could and then rushed off to tend to the *Paradise Ledger*. The relentless taunts of the other folks in town reverberated in Abby's mind. *Her father is probably glad that she's so homely. That way no one will ever want to marry her, and she can take care of him forever.*

Abby knew that her father loved her, but he just couldn't put it into words. For a man that made his living as a writer, you'd think he would be better at communicating. Abby's thoughts turned back to a time when she was younger–when even her distracted father thought she was too young to leave at home when he went away in search of his ghosts and shadows.

Abby's eyes fluttered open and she stared into her father's face. He looked so sad. Didn't he know that proving the existence of ghosts would never make him happy? They'd traveled across the country to this creepy town and in all that time they had hardly said anything real to one another. It had been like this since Abby's mother died from smallpox a year ago. Last month her father was obsessed with secret societies and now it was ghosts. Who could say what would be next?

"What time is it?" Abby asked. She propped herself up on her elbows, yawning furiously.

"Almost six o'clock," said her father. He removed a watch from his vest, checked the time, and then slipped it back into his pocket. "I've got the camera set up. You'd better get moving if you want to see."

"The ghost?"

Her father stared at her as if this was the most ordinary thing in the world. "Of course," he said. "Come on."

Sighing heavily, making sure that her father could hear her frustration, Abby crawled from the bed of the wagon and followed him toward the squatty little build-ing they had traveled so far to see. A cold rain began to fall as they crossed the grassy expanse that once held the Federal Armory,

Abby tested the doorknob in her attic prison. It turned easily and the door opened just a crack. She shut it. She had done this a hundred times since Farnum stuck her away up here. He hadn't even bothered to lock the door. He knew about their attempted escape from the Anderson place—he was there when Frank Avery dragged them back like two scolded hounds.

"I don't know if you're planning to run," Farnum had said, "but I wouldn't advise it."

That was all he said. No threats or anything to indicate what would happen to her if she opened that door and crept down the stairs. She was bound by her fear and she wasn't going anywhere.

"I heard something interesting," her father said as they sat in the doorway of the firehouse. Rain had been

falling for half an hour now, but there was still no sign of the ghost.

"What's that?" Abby asked.

"One of the hostages that John Brown and his men captured was Lewis Washington, the great-grandnephew of George Washington."

"Oh."

Abby closed her eyes and breathed deeply. She wanted to grab her father by the arms and shout at him. "Mama is dead and now you're all I have left. I need you to tell me everything is going to be all right, but you won't even look at me. Can't you understand how alone I feel?"

Her father smiled as he became lost in his storytelling. "Apparently, Lewis Washington had a sword that once belonged to his famous relative. John Brown captured the sword and was wearing it during most of the standoff."

Abby wasn't listening. Her eyes moved across the green to a man-shaped figure moving briskly down the abandoned street. "Who's that?" she asked.

Her father strained his eyes, trying to make out the approaching figure.

"Papa?" Abby said, a note of fear in her voice. She closed her cold hands around his arm and pulled herself close to him.

The apparition drew nearer, and Abby recognized him at once from the newspaper clippings her father had shown her on the train ride from Colorado. Tall and broad-shouldered, his mad eyes wide with holy fervor, a man who looked impossibly like the infamous John Brown was walking toward the firehouse. His unkempt hair and squared-off beard were unaffected by the drizzling rain. They remained dry, as did his clothes, which were at least twenty-five years out of fashion.

"It's him!" Webb shouted. "It's really him!" Taking a step backward, her father instinctively positioned Abby out of the direct path of the ghost.

Abby's heart thundered as the ghost crossed the street and began his trek across the grassy lawn. She could feel tension in her father's arms, and when she realized that he was also afraid, Abby's terror doubled. She knew little about the man whose ghost they had come to photograph. She'd heard the song, of course; everybody knew the song. 'John Brown's body lies a-mouldrin' in the grave, but his soul goes marching on.' Whoever wrote those words probably had no idea how true they really were.

"Papa!" Abby shouted. "He's coming this way. What do we do?" Suddenly all the tension that had been developing between father and daughter over the past year simply vanished. Gone was the shame Abby felt when she had to explain to the other children in the schoolhouse about her father's unusual job. Even the lingering sorrow that had shadowed Abby's heart ever since her mother slipped into the sleep of death was momentarily forgotten. All that mattered was this moment. Her father dragged her halfway across the country to find a ghost and prove to the world, and to his daughter, that he hadn't lost his mind.

And now, in the crumbling ruins of this firehouse, her father had done just that.

"Abby!" Webb shouted. "Take the picture!"

Moving with an inner strength she didn't know she possessed, Abby positioned herself behind the camera that was already aimed at the doorway.

Abby couldn't keep from trembling as the ghost of John Brown stepped through the doorway into the firehouse. The apparition's eyes seemed troubled…sorrowful. Her father told her his theory, that ghosts were spirits that had returned from the grave to a place that had been a source of great emotional trauma in their lives. There couldn't have been a more haunting place than *this in the life of John Brown. It was here, at Harpers Ferry, that Brown lost most of his small force of freedom fighters, including two of his own sons. And this was only the latest tragedy in a life that had been full of death and disappointment. It was no wonder then that John Brown's troubled spirit should choose to return to the setting of his ultimate defeat.*

Brown's eyes met her father's as the ghost entered the firehouse. They stared at each other across a gulf of years and history and metaphysical understanding. "Without the shedding of blood," those eyes seemed to convey, "there is no remission from sin."

"Take the picture!" Webb shouted.

The camera flashed, and when her eyes adjusted once more to the darkness, Abby saw that John Brown's ghost had vanished.

There was an old steamer trunk in the attic–the kind with wooden slats and rusted, brass hardware. Abby had circled around and around the thing since Farnum stuck her in here, but the idea of going through someone else's belongings was repellent to her. As the hours went by, however, as the heat pressed in on her, she stopped caring about right and wrong.

Abby knelt before the trunk and flipped open the two big latches that held it shut. She opened the lid and a hint of perfume filled her nostrils. There was a well-worn Bible resting atop a folded, white dress. She opened the Bible and turned past a few pages of hand-written genealogy before her eyes settled on a familiar name. She read:

Jeremy Farnum married Rebecca Tapp, May 18 1873. Offspring: Eunice, b. July 19, 1875, d. July 21, 1875. Georgiana, b. February 6, 1877, d. February 12, 1877. Walter, b. June15, 1888.

"I lost two girls," said an unfamiliar voice.

Abby dropped the Bible back on top of the dress. It didn't matter that she was the one locked up here like Bertha Mason in *Jane Eyre*, snooping through someone else's things just felt wrong. When Abby turned around, she saw a bony woman with long, black hair standing before her. She was Rebecca Farnum, Jeremy's wife.

"I... I'm sorry," Abby said. "I didn't hear you..."

Rebecca smiled wanly. "They were born sick, my girls. Poor little things."

Abby stared at the woman, unsure what she should say. There were tears in Mrs. Farnum's eyes.

"It ain't right that he's keeping you locked away up here," said Rebecca.

Abby nodded.

"It ain't right, but..." she took a step toward Abby, gently touching the girl's hair with the tips of her fingers. "I wonder what my girls would have looked like if they got the chance to grow up?"

"You could let me out of here," Abby said. "Make your husband let..."

Rebecca let out a sound that might have been a laugh. It was terrible. "No one makes Jeremy do anything." The woman stroked Abby's hair again. "Your father should have kept his nose out of other people's business."

Abby shrugged away from Rebecca. "My father is a newspaperman. His business is the truth."

Rebecca laughed again. "Truth?" she asked. "What is truth?"

The echo of her father's oft repeated maxim plucked at Abby's heartstrings. Joshua Webb's search for truth had taken him all over the country, but what had it ever brought their family but sorrow?

She struggled against her tears, not wanting to show weakness in front of Mrs. Farnum.

"I'm sorry about all this," Rebecca said. "You seem like a nice girl... I'll bring you up something to eat."

"I'm not hungry."

Rebecca took one last long look at Abby and then walked away. Abby paused beside the steamer trunk for a moment and then closed the lid. She sat down on top of the trunk and thought back to the trip she took to Harpers Ferry with her father five years earlier.

Abby sat on the edge of her bed in a room in the Hilltop Hotel later that day. The view of Harpers Ferry was amazing, but Abby hardly noticed. She waited in desperate anticipation as her father developed the photograph she had taken of John Brown's ghost. Abby was starting to worry that something was wrong. When her father emerged from his makeshift darkroom, the look on his face told her that she was right.

"Papa?" she asked. "What is it?"

"The photograph," Webb said. Disappointment was evident in his voice.

"*Let me see.*"

Webb handed his daughter the photograph, and Abby saw right away what her father was talking about. In spite of her fear that she had somehow done something wrong, the image was perfectly clear. She could plainly see the walls and the open door of the firehouse, and her father's frantic expression as he turned toward the camera. The only thing missing was the ghost. In the place where John Brown should have been, Abby saw only a blurry haze.

"*I don't understand,*" *she said.* "*What happened?*"

"*I don't know,*" *said Webb. He sat down heavily on the bed.* "*We had everything set up, we should have photographic evidence right now. Instead all we have is the same thing we started with…nothing.*"

Abby's eyes moved from the photograph to her father. In spite of her disappointment, a smile began to form at the corners of Abby's lips. No, she thought, we have something else.

"*I'm sorry, Papa,*" *Abby said as tenderly as she could. Her father turned to her but said nothing. Abby reached for him, closing a small hand on his left wrist.* "*I know it probably doesn't mean much,*" *she whispered,* "*but I want to thank you for bringing me here with you. Even if no one else believes you, I saw that ghost with my own eyes, and I want you to know that I believe in you."*

Joshua Webb turned toward his daughter, his eyes glistening with emotion. When he spoke, his voice cracked. "You're wrong," he said. "It means everything." He wrapped an arm around his daughter and pulled her close.

Outside, the storm continued unabated, baptizing the sleepy village of Harpers Ferry with purifying rain from Heaven.

★ ★ ★ CHAPTER 11 ★ ★ ★
THE GATHERING STORM

The residents of Paradise called the place Browntown, but it wasn't their intention to be hurtful. This was where all the colored folks lived–former slaves and their offspring who had taken up Horace Greely's invitation to go west, but who had found there only more of the same kinds of people that had driven them out of the east. Browntown was a collection of ramshackle houses and shops tucked away a mile or so outside of Paradise proper. It was there–away from the prying eyes of his neighbors, any of whom could be in Jeremy Farnum's employ–that Joshua Webb brought the battered shell of the woman he loved.

Elizabeth McLarty lay in a bed in the back room of the Shinbone house, her eye wide and vacant as she stared, unblinking, at the ceiling overhead.

"Is she..."

"She's gonna have a rough go of it," said Mercy Shinbone, a midwife who had delivered Abby when she was born. Sarah always liked the woman, and given the situation with the widow, she was about the only person in town that Webb could trust.

"I never should have put her in this situation," he said. He was heartsick over what had happened to Elizabeth, and the thought of his daughter in the hands of those monsters chilled him to the bone.

"No," said Mercy. "You should have been there to protect her instead of gallavanting all over..."

"Mercy!"

Rance Shinbone, Mercy's husband, hushed his wife with a single word, but Webb knew what she meant. All of this was his fault and he knew it. He had no business chasing conspiracy theories and secret societies... he was a father and if he weren't such a fool, he might be a husband again as well. The *Paradise Ledger* had cost him so much already, but after Sarah died it was something he could throw himself into—something he could do instead of feeling the terrible emptiness that lay beside him in the bed at night.

Mercy met her husband's eyes with a look that could have melted glass, but she let the subject drop. After a moment her eyes shifted back to Webb. "I'll do my best to take care of the widow," she said. "You can just leave her here and try to find your girl."

Webb bowed his head, ashamed that he had allowed this situation to come to pass.

"Ranse here will be happy to help you," she said. "Won't you love?"

"Yes, ma'am," said Ranse. Webb had seen Ranse shoot before–he was damned good–but too many people had already suffered because of Boston Corbett and the Society of the Cincinnati. Webb didn't want the Shinbone's to be dragged down as well.

"The two of you have proven to be good friends to me," Webb said. "Better than I deserve. But you have a family here and the last thing I want to do is to get you all tangled up in my troubles."

Ranse looked from his wife to the editor. "You say that Jeremy Farnum has your girl, ain't that right?"

"That's right."

"A girl that my Mercy here helped bring into the world?"

Webb nodded.

"Seems to me," said Ranse," that we're already tangled up in your troubles Mister Webb."

The editor nodded solemnly. "Thank you," he said, "but I must insist. Farnum is involved with some sort of... secret society... you can see as well as I that they're dangerous."

Ranse moved to a bureau in the corner of the room and retrieved a Sharps' carbine that was leaning against the wall. He looked at Webb with the eyes of a hunter. "Let's go get your girl, Mister Webb."

Corbett and Anders were waiting outside the house. They had accompanied Webb when he brought Elizabeth here, though neither man had said a word during that nightmare journey. Anders looked the same as always–ruddy-faced and ready to pester the girls at the *Paradise Theater* for a poke. Corbett looked like walking death. The wound in his arm was bleeding again and his shirt was a bloody mess. His skin was pale and there were dark circles around his eyes.

"How is she?" Anders said.

"Bad."

"Joshua... I'm sorry I... Corbett wouldn't meet Webb's eyes when he spoke. Maybe he was feeling guilty about everything that had happened. It was his letters after all that kindled this trouble. There was a part of Webb that wanted to lay all of the blame on Boston Corbett, but he knew in his heart that this idea was false.

"You need a doctor, Mister," Webb said.

"I don't think that's a good idea," said Corbett.

"No, I don't suppose that it is." If the man who shot John Wilkes Booth entered Paradise he would be captured by Farnum and his men almost at once. Corbett's only hope for freedom was to remain at large.

"You should hand me over to the Society. Maybe Farnum will exchange me for your daughter."

Did he mean it? Webb stared at him for a long moment. "Too much has happened and I don't believe they would let either of us see the light of day again."

"Then you understand the ways of the Society," said Corbett. "They do not value life over the ends of their schemes and plans."

"Where are we going?" Anders asked.

Webb climbed up beside the man in the buck-board they had commandeered from Frank Avery. Elizabeth's assailant, the agent of The Society, lay face down in the dirt with Anders' bullet in his back. As far as Webb was concerned, the buzzards could have him.

"First to my place," Webb said, "and then I'm going to pay a visit to Jeremy Farnum. If that bastard has hurt my girl I'm going to put a bullet between his eyes."

Ranse climbed into the back of the wagon with Corbett. He was settling down as Anders took up the reins and they drove off into the dusky afternoon.

I hate guns, Webb thought as they rolled along through the trees. *I haven't touched one since Washita.* The things he saw during those terrible years haunted him still. Sioux, Apache, Cheyenne... it got so that killing became almost routine. He swore off violence after Washita, but Abby was his little girl and there was only so much that a man could tolerate.

I don't want to hurt anyone, he thought, *but I'll do it if I have to.* He didn't care if it was Jeremy Farnum or Grover Cleveland himself, he aimed to get his daughter back no matter the cost.

Life went on as normal in Paradise. Men gathered to drink and play cards at the *Paradise Theater*. Women did their shopping at Reynolds Mercantile. Children sat in neat rows in the schoolhouse, staring dreamily out the windows and wishing that it was time for recess. These sturdy folk, the salt of the earth, had no concept of the events unfolding in their midst. They were sheep, wholly unaware that a wolf was among them.

Colonel Price had chased Boston Corbett and his accomplice all the way from Topeka, knowing full-well that he would find his quarry in Paradise. The Army kept excellent records, and the contents of every piece of mail that Corbett sent or received had been cataloged by the staff of the Topeka State Hospital. The man who had aided Corbett's escape was Joshua Webb, a newspaper editor and something of a pariah to the people of this town. All the colonel had to do was find Webb and he would find Corbett. The man who shot John Wilkes Booth was the bait, and once he was back in custody, Price and his superiors could spring the trap they had been constructing for years.

First things first, the colonel made his way to the Sheriff's office as soon as he and his men arrived in town. Price opened the door and found Sheriff Tom Watters sitting at his desk, absently twisting the ends of his black mustache. A single jail cell filled up a quarter of the room, but it was empty. For now. Maybe later, when the booze started flowing and the miners from up in the hills came in for their evening poke, things would be different, but for now Paradise was at peace.

A small-framed man was sitting across from the sheriff, wringing his hands nervously as he sat slumped in his chair. He was complaining about all the Chinese that were in the area because of the railroad, but he stopped talking as soon as Price entered the room. Both men turned to look at the colonel.

"Sheriff Watters? I'm Colonel Price with the U.S. Army. I need to speak to you in private. It's an urgent matter."

Watters looked from the colonel to Jake. The small man had an annoyed expression on his face, but it didn't matter one bit to the colonel. He was here with the authority of the United States government, and that of another power even greater.

"Mister Slicker," said the Sheriff, "if you'll excuse us..."

The small man stood slowly, glared once at Price, and then fled the office without a word.

The officer sat down in the recently vacated chair and reached into his coat pocket. He removed a carte de visite and slid it across the desk toward the sheriff. "Have you seen this man?" he asked.

Watters retrieved the photograph and took a hard look. The photo showed a slender man in an Army uniform leaning against a fancy carved chair. His dark hair was parted right down the middle and he wore a mustache and scraggly beard. His eyes were gaunt, like those of a man who is haunted by some deep trouble. "Who is he?" asked the Sheriff.

Price leaned forward, his elbows resting on the edge of Watters' desk. "Sheriff, what I'm about to tell you is a matter of national security."

"Oh?"

"We have reason to believe that a dangerous outlaw is hiding out here in Paradise. This man has connections to a group dedicated to the overthrow of the Union."

"You can't be serious."

The colonel's eyes narrowed dramatically. "Someone broke him out of prison in Topeka," he said, "and we believe they arrived in Paradise on yesterday's train."

"What's his name?" asked the sheriff.

"Boston Corbett."

"The man who shot John Wilkes Booth? He's a hero."

Price shook his head slowly. "No sir. He's a madman, and the lives of every person in this town are at risk until he's back in my custody. And that's just the least of it. I need your help, Sheriff. The very future of this nation is at risk."

The buckboard stopped at the little white church on the hill. They could see all of Paradise from here—the clutch of buildings on Main Street, the houses of the folks that lived in town, the outlying farms that supplied the food for the townsfolk, and the cluster of homes that comprised Browntown. They could even see the big house where Jeremy Farnum lived... where Webb's daughter was surely being held at this very moment. This was the battlefield where the war with Society of the Cincinnati would be waged. Not out in the middle of a wheat field like they did it back in the Civil War but right here on the street of Paradise.

They had been out to Webb's house and retrieved a small stash of weapons that the editor kept in an old trunk in the barn. A Sharp's carbine, a Colt Peacemaker and an army cutlass... these were the tools of the soldier Webb had been in his previous life. They collected dust while he waged war with his newspaper, but the time for ink had come to an end. Now was the time for blood.

"You should stay right here," said Webb, his eyes falling heavily on Corbett. "I don't know that you'll be safe, but you're no use to us in your condition and I want to keep you as far away from Farnum as possible."

Corbett nodded solemnly as he eyed the church. "I will dwell in the house of The Lord forever," he said. He climbed down from the wagon and walked slowly up the church. He turned back once, lifted a hand as if in farewell, and then pushed open the door. It was the last time he would lay eyes on the man in this life. When Corbett was safely inside the church, Webb turned to Ranse.

"That man is the only bargaining chip that I have," he said. "I need you to watch over him. Can you do that?"

Ranse's eyes narrowed. "You want me to stay here?"

"If something happens to him, I'll never see Abby again. I can't even be sure that he will stay put once we roll out of sight."

"You might need my gun when you get to Farnum's ranch," Ranse said. "He has a bunch of rough hombres working out at his place."

"You're probably right," said Webb. "But I need you here even more."

Ranse jumped down from the wagon. "You watch your back," he said. "I might just say a prayer for you and Harris, while I'm waiting."

"I'd appreciate that." Webb tipped his hat at the farmer as the buckboard pulled away. The sun was going down on Paradise.

CHAPTER 12

MANIFEST DESTINY

The Farnum Ranch was majestic by all accounts. From the columns and the two-tiered front porch to the gabled roof, the huge white house was a symbol to the people of Paradise, Colorado that Jeremy Farnum was wealthy and powerful and not to be trifled with. He was superior to them in every way and he wanted them to know it.

"What are you gonna do?" Harris Anders asked. "Walk right up to the front door and ask to see Jeremy Farnum?"

There were two figures standing on a hill overlooking the Farnum Ranch. Joshua Webb and Harris Anders; the soldier and the trapper. They looked down upon their quarry like an Indian raiding party about to ambush their prey.

"Something like that," Webb said. "Come on."

As far as plans went, there wasn't much to go on. There was a bunkhouse on the property where Farnum's men—the cowboys that did all the labor on his ranch—took their meals and spent their evenings drinking rot gut when they didn't have the money for an evening at the *Paradise Theater*. Webb and Anders watched as the cook appeared through the bunkhouse's single door and began banging on dinner bell as if he had some sort of personal grudge against the thing. Cowboys came trickling in from all over the ranch, and after a few minutes, it seemed to Webb that they were all accounted for.

The editor turned to Anders. "You guard the door," he said. "You can likely keep the lot of them tied up in there with some big talk and a well-placed shot or two."

"Pretty likely," Anders agreed.

"Don't kill anyone," said Webb, "not unless you have to."

The trapper chambered a bullet into his rifle. "You be careful up at the big house. Might be more trouble there than you're bargaining for."

Webb left his companion behind and moved silently along the tree line. There were lights on in the big house–the word around town was that Farnum had some of those new electric lights. The editor heard voices inside as he approached the house. He wondered if he would be forced to silence any of those voices before the night was done. He touched the handle of his saber as he walked slowly up the dusky path. He was willing to do whatever it took to bring Abby home.

The editor climbed the stairs onto the porch and slammed the knocker on the door three times. The door opened wide and a thin man with a clean face appeared in the opening. His dark hair was receding and would be all white within a year or two. He wore a fine, dark suit that was less threadbare than the one Webb was wearing.

"How may I..." said Farnum's butler, but Webb kicked him in the gut and sent the man sprawling backward into the house. He drew his saber and shoved through the door.

"Farnum!" Webb cried. "I want to talk to you, you son of a bitch."

The butler reached for a Derringer that was strapped to his ankle, but the editor stomped on the man's hand, breaking his fingers. Webb kicked the small gun and it went skidding across the floorboards.

"Farnum!" He shouted again.

A door slammed open down the hall and Jeremy Farnum appeared with a pistol in his hand. He raised the weapon, but he was a businessman, not a gun-slinger, and Webb was a trained soldier. He drew his Peacemaker and fired before Farnum could react. The rich man's gun went flying as Farnum grabbed his now injured hand. He was wearing a fancy waist-coat over a starched white shirt. This was the first time Webb had ever seen the man without his coat, but it was hot here in Paradise–as hot as Hell some might say.

"What the Hell is this about?" Farnum demanded.

"Where is she?" said Webb. He could feel the anger boiling inside of him, and it took every mea-sure of self-control that he possessed not to gun this man down right in his own foyer. But if he did, he was certain that he would never see Abby again. The editor holstered his gun and took a step toward Farnum, saber in hand.

"I-I don't know what you're talking about," Farnum said.

"My daughter. I know you've taken her."

Farnum held up his hands, palms open, as if here were trying to ward off an impending blow. "Mister Webb, I assure you..."

Webb's hand flew before he knew what was happening. He punched Farnum in the face with the saber's knuckle bow, shattering his nose. The man in white staggered backward, crashing into a mirror mounted on the wall behind him. Webb caught a glimpse of himself in the mirror as it fell, shattering into a thousand shards when it hit the floor. He looked like a mad man, like someone that belonged in the Topeka State Hospital.

The butler, still clenching his broken hand, was staring at him in disbelief as Webb leaned over Farnum, grabbed a fistful of the rich man's shirt and pulled him up off the ground. There were cuts all over his face and his nose was ruined. Webb didn't care. This was nothing compared to what he had done at Washita, and he was more than willing to send this man to his death. After what had happened to Elizabeth, death was too good for Jeremy Farnum.

Webb dropped his saber. It clattered on the floor boards as the editor drew his pistol and shoved the barrel under Farnum's jaw. "I'm not going to ask you again, Farnum. Where's Abby?" Webb pulled back the hammer with an audible click.

"I told you," Farnum said through gritted teeth, "I don't know."

"Don't make me kill you, Farnum."

There was a commotion behind him, and Webb turned just enough to see the butler scurrying out the front door. Going to warn the boys in the bunkhouse, he figured. Webb hoped that Anders would be able to keep that lot occupied.

"I'll find her," Webb said, "if I have to tear this house down brick by..."

"Papa?"

The voice came from the top of the stairs. When Webb looked up he saw the child, a blonde-haired boy leaning over the stair rail, his eyes wide with fear for his father. A frail woman stood beside the boy, holding him tight. From this angle, it appeared that the only thing keeping the boy from falling to his death was Rebecca Farnum's tiny, pale hand.

"What are you doing to my Papa?" cried the boy.

Oh, God, Webb thought. The sight of the boy brought him instantly back to Washita, to the massacre of women and children in which he had participated along with the rest of Custer's men. He had spilled innocent blood in the name of Manifest Destiny, but no matter how many times he quoted John O'Sullivan, it could never wash the blood from off of his hands. Time had lightened that burden, if only by a little bit, but Webb wasn't sure that he was ready to blow Farnum's head off right in front of his son.

Farnum's wife didn't say a word, she just stared at him with her cold eyes betraying no emotion whatsoever. Webb turned back to Farnum's ruined face. His eyes burned with hatred as they stared out of his crimson mask, and his fancy white clothes were stained with blood.

"I don't care what happens to me," said Webb. "I don't care about the Ledger or Boston Corbett or the United States of America. I want my girl and I want her back. I know that you want Corbett... fine. I've got him hidden out and I will trade him to you for my girl. Now, tell me where you've hidden my girl."

Harris Anders heard the gunshot inside the big house, but no one in the bunkhouse seemed to notice. It sounded like quite a shindig in there. Anders thought about the unusual string of events that had led him from a pleasant evening at the brothel to standing out here listening to Farnum's cowboys devouring their supper. As a trapper, Anders spent considerable time alone in the woods, and a man could get powerful lonely leading a life like that. He drank too much, he knew, but his time in the wilderness kept him dry and he figured to make up for it when he was in town. And there was nothing like the softness of a woman when a man was in his cups.

Anders was thinking about a girl he used to know–a pretty little thing with yellow hair and porcelain skin–when a man came shrieking out of the darkness. He was clutching his right hand to his chest like a little girl holding her favorite doll, and there were tears on the man's cheeks.

"Trouble in the house," he shouted. "Come on, you fools, Mister Farnum needs you."

The man didn't notice Anders as he ran up to the bunkhouse door. He was shouting like a madman and banging on the door with his good hand for a full minute before the cook finally opened the door.

"What is it?" he demanded.

Anders raised his rifle and took aim at the dinner bell hanging beside the men's heads. He pulled the trigger. There was a loud bang, and almost instantaneously, the dinner bell rang out.

"You boys just stay put and finish your supper," Anders said. His voice bellowed out of the darkness like a preacher on Sunday morning. "Y'all are surrounded and I hate to have to shoot anyone."

"Who's there?" said the cook. "Is this some kind of joke?"

"Ain't no joke," Anders said.

The injured man, Farnum's butler, leaned in close and whispered something to the cook.

"Talk all you like," Anders said, "so long as you do it in that there bunkhouse."

"How many of you are there?" asked the cook.

"Enough."

"What does that crazy editor want with Mister Farnum?"

He's buying time, Anders realized. They must have another way out of the bunkhouse. He wished that Ranse was here instead of back at that church sitting on his hands. Another gun might prove damn useful in the next few minutes.

"Your boss has Mister Webb's little girl held prisoner," Anders said. "And he did quite a number on the Widow McLarty."

The trapper tensed as the shadows moved around him. Someone was out here with him, he was sure of it.

"I wouldn't mess with Mister Farnum if I was you," said the cook.

Anders pulled the trigger and rang the dinner bell a second time. The sound was still ringing in his ears when the trapper felt the bullet enter his back. He crumpled to his knees as his rifle fell from his lifeless fingers. Harris Anders fell face-first into the leaves, his eyes staring blankly into the darkness. He was dead.

Webb heard a gunshot in the yard outside and the sound of the dinner bell ringing. Something was happening out there, but he couldn't worry about that now.

"I told you already," said Farnum, "I have no idea what you're talking about." He gasped with each word, his ruined nose forcing him to breath through his mouth. "The last time I saw your daughter was in town..."

Webb drew back his pistol and was about to bludgeon Farnum with the butt of the gun when a shadow darkened his vision. The editor turned toward the front door and saw a dark-eyed cowboy standing there. He had a rifle pressed to his shoulder that looked an awful lot like the one that belonged to Harris Anders.

"Drop your gun," said the cowboy. His lips parted in a grin, revealing a mouth full of blackened teeth.

One question rang out in Webb's mind: could he drop this cowboy before the dark-eyed man filled him full of lead? He knew at once that the answer was no. Webb took one last look at Farnum and then dropped his pistol to the floor. A second cowboy appeared behind the first–another hired gun that looked like he would be willing to shoot a man for a dollar.

Farnum pulled himself to his feet beside the editor. He spat blood on Webb's boots and then stepped uncomfortably close to the man.

"I have every right to shoot you," he whispered. "I could give the order and young Elmer here would be happy to oblige."

"That's right," said the dark-eyed cowboy.

"Do it," Webb said, "and you'll never see Boston Corbett again."

Farnum licked his teeth and then spat blood again. "You're not going to do your girl any good bleeding to death on my floor."

"So you have seen her then?"

The man in white grinned a terrible grin. "Come on, boys," he said. "Bring him outside. I don't want to spill any more blood on the carpet."

The second cowboy took Webb by the arm and dragged him through the front door. He caught one last glimpse of Rebecca Farnum and her boy, still watching from the top of the stairs. There was no emotion on the woman's face–this might have been a theatrical performance starring Edwin Booth. Her husband was bleeding all over the place but she didn't seem to care how the story unfolded. And the boy... he watched his father with worshipful eyes. How long would it be before that boy began walking in his father's footsteps? The thought chilled Webb to his bones.

There were no lights burning in the old church, just a hint of moonlight spilling through the windows. The people of Paradise were a practical lot, not finding it necessary to invest in stained glass and a lot of fancy ornamentation. Boston Corbett sat in the third row from the front, his hands clasped before him and his eyes shut tightly to the world outside. He had been praying for hours, ever since Editor Webb left him here. His clothes were soaked with blood, but he hardly noticed. He was communing with The Lord and nothing else in this world mattered.

"Father God," Corbett said, "what have I done? I put an innocent family in jeopardy, and cost a good woman her virtue."

Silence weighed heavily in the empty church.

"I know there is none good but you," Corbett said. "All the same, I am full of sorrows."

"There is a great event before you," said a disembodied voice.

Corbett opened his eyes in the near darkness. He was alone save for a crucified Christ mounted on the wall above the pulpit.

"Its arrival is certain," said the voice. "It will sunder all your relations to the present world and break every tie of mortality..."

Corbett stood up in the pews. He scanned the darkened sanctuary, trying to figure out who was speaking. It sounded like the Voice of God to the man who shot John Wilkes Booth.

"Strip off every disguise. Expose every error and deception. Bring to light every secret thing."

The front doors of the church opened wide and silvery moonlight poured into the room. The figure of a man stood silhouetted in the doorway. It appeared to Corbett that this was an angel, or perhaps Jesus Christ himself, come to palaver with his humble servant. Corbett prostrated himself before the avatar of The Lord.

"Lord, Lord," he said as tears streamed down his face. "The tie that binds me to the earth is as frail as a flower. The wind passeth over, and it will soon be gone. Will you bless me before I die?"

The face of The Lord stared at Corbett without recognition. "I never knew you," he said.

Those were the worst words that a Christian could hear in his time of judgement. They struck Boston Corbett like a shot from a cannon. His mind wandered backward across the life he had led—a life full of violence and death. Had he ever truly known The Lord or was everything he had done in vain?

"Have I not prophesied in thy name?" Corbett asked. "And in thy name cast out devils and done many wonderful works?"

"Depart from me, ye cursed, into everlasting fire, prepared for the devil and his angels."

Corbett felt his heart breaking as The Lord spoke his damnation. His shoulders heaved as he wept on the dusty floor of a church without even a name.

"For I was hungered," said the voice of The Lord, "and ye gave me no meat: I was thirsty, and ye gave me no drink. I was a stranger, and ye took me not in: naked, and ye clothed me not: sick, and in prison, and ye visited me not."

Corbett balled his left hand into a fist and punched the wooden floor with all his might. His knuckles fractured–his tears and his blood pooled on the boards beneath him.

"Lord," he cried, "when did I see thee hungered, or athirst, or a stranger, or naked, or sick, or in prison, and did not minister unto thee?" He closed his eyes, and the last thing he saw before the darkness claimed him were the bare, nail-scarred feet of his master.

"Verily I say unto you," spoke the avatar of The Lord, "Inasmuch as ye did it not to one of the least of these, ye did it not to me."

"Corbett? Are you okay?" said a man dressed in the plain clothes and worn-out shoes of a farmer. Ranse Shinbone knelt beside Corbett, who lay in a pool of his own blood. "Corbett? Wake up you..."

Ranse felt for a heartbeat in the dying man's neck. It was there, but just barely. Webb had tasked him with protecting Corbett from Farnum and his men, but there was nothing he could do about the man's injuries. A wound he had received a few days earlier had reopened, and the man who shot John Wilkes Booth was dying of the blood poisoning. There was only one thing Ranse could do... he had to go for the doctor.

CHAPTER 13

SLIPKNOT

Webb's first thought, when he saw the big maple, was that they were going to hang him. Farnum's men drug him across the yard and shoved him to the ground at the base of the tree. He started to rise, but the dark-eyed cowboy kicked Webb in the face before he could gain his footing. The editor crumpled, his vision going momentarily black.

They bound his hands together at the wrists and then draped a slipknot over his hands. The other end of the rope was tossed over a high branch and then Webb felt his body being lifted and stretched. He opened his eyes and saw the cowboys pulling on the rope and tying it off. Webb's toes dangled just inches off the ground, but he could not find purchase. He was strung up like a hog ready to be butchered. He closed his eyes and tried not throw up. His head was swimming and the way the rope swayed was making it worse. It helped to clench his eyes shut, but not much. He thought of Abby and tried to remain focused.

The man in white approached slowly, his boots crunching gravel with every step. "I've read your little newspaper," Farnum said. "It's trash. Secret societies and government cabals... no one believes the lies you spin in the *Paradise Ledger*."

Webb's boots scraped at the dirt and he twisted back and forth in the night.

"This is quite a story you've stumbled upon," Farnum continued. "But no one in his right mind would believe you if you printed it. You know that, don't you?"

Webb didn't answer. What could he possibly say?

Farnum rolled up the sleeves of his soiled white shirt, exposing his well-muscled forearms. He struck out suddenly, punching the editor in his exposed stomach with brutal force. Webb hung there, gasping for air, as Farnum leaned in close.

"Your girl is upstairs right now, watching you suffer." He said it in a whisper, and then stepped back, his voice returning to normal. "Everyone in this town thinks you are a fool, Mister Webb. Isn't that right, boys?"

The cowboys laughed sardonically, but Webb didn't care about them. Farnum's words cut him deeply, but they also offered a glimmer of hope. If Abby was up there, watching, that meant she was alive.

One of the cowboys handed something to Farnum. It looked like a snake, and it took a moment for Webb's rattled brain to process what it was. A bullwhip.

"You have no idea what you've stumbled into," Farnum said. "You should have minded your own business."

He cracked the whip one time and the sound rang in Webb's ears like a church bell. He braced himself for what was about to happen, but there was no amount of preparedness that would help. There was another crack, and the editor's shirt was torn open from collar to waist.

Webb screamed; he couldn't help it.

The whip cracked again.

And again.

And again.

Joshua Webb thought in the narrative voice. Whatever was happening in his life, whatever he saw, his mind described it like a story.

Once upon a time, there was a man who believed in truth.

This man wrote the truth and everyone laughed. He was called a lunatic. A heretic. A madman.

He traveled the country in search of truth, but what he found was a secret society that worshipped their own lies.

They tried to break this man.

They assaulted an innocent woman. They kidnapped the man's daughter.

I am that man.

Webb faded in and out of consciousness as his punishment endured. He lost track of the time.

"Cut him down," Farnum said.

When the dark-eyed cowboy drew his knife, the editor thought his tormenters were going to end it, but Farnum's man stretched out the blade and cut the ropes that were binding Webb to the tree. He crashed to the ground with a thud, and pain erupted through the editor's mutilated back. He would bear the scars for the rest of his life, however long that might be.

"Maybe we should call the coroner," said one of the cowboys. He leaned over Webb and cut the ropes from his wrists.

Webb was lifted to a kneeling position, and then Farnum grabbed him by the hair and leaned in close. His breath smelled like coffee and his nose was badly swollen. One of his eyes was blackened and that gave Webb just a hint of satisfaction.

"If you ever want to see your girl again," said Farnum in a whisper, "you'll tell me where I can find Boston Corbett."

Webb tried to focus on the man, but his eyes refuse to cooperate. "I offered... to trade..." he said. "Why..."

"You broke into my home and assaulted me," said Farnum. "No one does that. No one."

"You took... my girl. Hurt Eliz..."

"And now you know what I am capable of. Now you know that there is no line I will not cross."

Webb bowed his head. He understood.

"You're gonna take me to Corbett," said Farnum, "and that's all there is to it. Am I right?"

"You're right," Webb said.

"Where is he?"

Webb took a deep breath and closed his eyes. He said a silent prayer in mind, knowing full well that his one hope of rescuing Abby was slipping from his fingers. He opened his eyes and spit the bitter words from his mouth. "He's at the church."

"Fine. That's just fine. Now, I'm going to get cleaned up and then you and I are going to take a ride in my surrey." Farnum smiled and relaxed his grip. He nodded at his cowboys and they quickly set to work preparing the carriage.

Webb knelt in the grass, his back ruined and his heart broken as he waited for the man in white to emerge from the big house. This felt like an execution, and the noose was tightening around the editor's neck. He wondered if he would ever see his Abby again in this life, or if the next time they laid eyes on one another it would be in the world beyond the grave. He closed his eyes and prayed.

Colonel Price sat in the *Paradise Theater*, sipping a beer and reading the latest issue of the *Paradise Ledger*. The paper was several weeks old at this point, but sensational stories like the ones contained within didn't exactly need to be timely. The officer snick-ered as he finished an article about the supposed misdeeds of the Freemasons. Joshua Webb was like a lamb crying for its mother, but its mother wouldn't listen. Half of what he printed was nonsense, but the other half was the brutal truth. The only problem was that no one could tell which was which.

"Read something amusing?" asked Lieutenant Boone, Price's best man. Boone wore a neatly trimmed mustache and he was constantly pulling on the ends. It annoyed the Colonel to no end, but Boone was a capable soldier and he followed orders.

"This paper," Price said. "Joshua Webb must be the biggest fool in the territory."

He glanced out the window to the clinic across the street. He was never going to find Boston Corbett by searching all over town. The bulk of his men were doing just that, and thus far the only mention of any-one meeting Corbett's description was right here in the local whorehouse. That lead was actually pretty good, but Corbett was still on the loose so what did it matter?

Price took another sip of his beer. According to the lone soldier that survived, Corbett was injured during his escape from the Topeka State Hospital.

It was unfortunate that four good men were killed during the escape, but they were God's soldiers who had laid down their lives for the greater good. Perhaps his superiors should have foreseen that Corbett would turn violent given the opportunity, but it wasn't Price's place to judge those that God had seen fit to put over him. He had a job to do in Paradise, and there was no place for questioning orders.

This editor, Joshua Webb, struck Price as a curiosity. He served with General Custer in the Indian Wars, and, according to his records, he was part of the unit that took part in the infamous Washita Massacre. Price wondered if the blood on his hands had something to do with Webb's lunatic desire to seek out conspiracies and shadows everywhere he turned? The Colonel's superiors had been aware of Webb and the *Paradise Ledger* for some time, and he had played right into their hands when he helped Boston Corbett to escape. The fool ran right back home, and apparently tried to put up Corbett right here in this brothel. According to the witness here at the *Theater*, Corbett looked like he wasn't well. The Colonel figured that there was at least half a chance that the man who shot John Wilkes Booth would need the services of the town doctor before too long, and the clinic just happened to be located across from this fine establishment.

It was close to midnight when Price noticed the nigger rushing down the street and looking behind him like he was worried that someone was following him. How this stranger might fit into the story was beyond the Colonel, but it didn't matter. Corbett and Webb were probably hiding out there somewhere, and they might be using this fellow as a runner.

The man banged on the front door of the clinic and waited for several minutes until the town doctor appeared. He was a young man with a clean-shaven face. He spoke to the negro for a moment, nodded his head a few times, and then returned to the clinic to grab his medical bag. The two were off not ten minutes later, scurrying into the night like a couple of rats.

Price finished his beer, folded up the newspaper, and tucked it into his haversack. "Come on," he said to Boone, "Let's see what all the commotion is about."

They left the *Paradise Theater* and followed the doctor and the black man into the darkness. Price had a feeling, and his feelings rarely led him astray, that they were going to lead him straight to his quarry.

Farnum's surrey was luxury at its finest–a carriage worthy of the richest man in Paradise. Webb sat beside his adversary as Farnum drove his team of horses toward town. They rode in silence as Farnum navigated the surrey off of his property and onto the main road, the only sound that of the horses' hooves clopping on the dirt. It wasn't until they were well on their way that Farnum finally spoke.

"What did he tell you?"

"Corbett?"

"Who else?"

Webb thought back to the hours he and Corbett had spent sneaking around in the Kansas night... of the twisting tale Boston had told about John Wilkes Booth and the Society of the Cincinnati and the plot to murder Abraham Lincoln. "He told me about your secret society," said Webb. "About the strings you bastards are always pulling behind the scenes."

Farnum snickered.

"The Society of the Cincinnati," Webb continued, "architect of the Lincoln Assassination."

"That's lunacy," said Farnum. "We tried to protect Lincoln…"

"You trained John Wilkes Booth to be a cold-blooded killer, and organized a plot to overthrow the federal government."

"Booth wasn't one of our agents. We executed him for his actions. We avenged Lincoln's murder."

Webb wanted to the strangle Farnum for his lies, but he tempered his anger. Remaining calm was the only chance he had at ever seeing Abby again. "That's not what Corbett said. He told me all about his conditioning… about the cruel tortures you subjected him to. Stripping away a man's humanity and remaking him into monster."

"Would you consider Boston Corbett as a reliable source of information, Mister Webb? Are you planning to print this fantastic tale of secret societies and political intrigue in your newspaper?"

Webb stared at the road ahead as Paradise came into view. He thought about Abby and Elizabeth and all of the troubles that had come his way since he received that first letter from Boston Corbett . "I don't know," he said.

"Come on," Ranse said. "He passed out right in the church." He and the sawbones ran all the way from the clinic to the church, and Ranse was worried that Mister Webb's friend would be dead by the time they returned. They had just reached the little white church and were about to enter when they heard the unmistakable click of a pistol.

"Turn around real slow," said an unfamiliar voice. "And no tricks, Nigger, or I'll drop you dead."

Ranse could still remember the day when his grandmother came to him, tears streaming from her eyes, and said that they were free. He was only a boy, seven or eight years old, and he had no idea what she meant. His Grammy was crying, and he thought that meant something was wrong. She explained it to him, of course, and their little family huddled together in their cabin that night in the hills of Tennessee. They talked and dreamed long into the night of what the future would hold. As a child, still naive to the ways of the world, Ranse thought that all of his troubles were behind him. It wasn't until the shackles of slavery were broken off and he walked in the world as a free man that he realized that those shackles had only been replaced. He had a good life here in Paradise, a wife who loved him and children that would never be torn from his arms and sold away into bondage, but there would never be a time when men did not hate him because of the color of his skin. There would never be a time when trouble left him well enough alone. Here he was, trying to help out a friend, and there was a man pointing a gun at his back.

They turned to face their assailant, and Ranse was surprised to see two soldiers standing there. The younger of the two had a black mustache that was turned up on the ends. The older had a round face with a turned-up nose, and, sure enough, he was holding a pistol in his right hand. "I'm sure you have pressing business here," he said, "but I'm hoping you can take a minute to tell me what you're up to."

Doc Hostetler had an exasperated look on his face—he was one of the most respected men in town and he probably wasn't used to being treated like this. Ranse on the other hand...

"There's a man dying in there," said the doctor.

"Is that so?" The soldier reached into his pocked with his free hand and produced a ragged carte de visite. "Is this the man?"

"I have no idea," Hostetler said. "Mister Shinbone here just alerted me..."

"Why don't you take a look?"

Hostetler leaned forward cautiously, and took a gander at the picture. "I never seen him before in my life."

The soldier turned to Ranse. "What about you, Nigger? Have you seen him?"

Ranse suppressed his desire to attack this man. That would only end in his death, and what would Mercy and the children do without him? He wanted more than anything for his daughter and his son to live in a world where folks were judged by what they did, and not by the color of their skin or who their father was. He looked at the picture. It was Boston Corbett.

"I've never seen him..." Ranse began, but he knew that the soldier had seen the recognition in his face. He was never any good at hiding his emotions.

"Don't lie to me. That's him in there, ain't it?"

Ranse averted his eyes. He said nothing.

"The two of you had best skedaddle," said the soldier. "Go back to your lives and forget you were ever here. Boone, I want you to..."

A flash of anger crossed the doctor's face. "Are you going to go in there and murder a man in cold blood? This is God's house."

The soldier smiled, and the look chilled Ranse to the bone. "Unless you want to meet God personally, I'd suggest you get out of my sight."

The man called Boone took a step toward the church and Ranse and Hostetler parted before him like the sea in that story about the Children of Israel.

"We're going to report you to the sheriff," said the doctor as the soldier disappeared into the church.

"You do that," said the Colonel. "Now you both run along before I send you to The Lord above." He dismissed them with a wave of his pistol, and there was nothing Ranse and Hostetler could do but abandon Corbett to his fate.

★ ★ ★ CHAPTER 14 ★ ★ ★
THE LONESOME DEATH OF BOSTON CORBETT

The interloper crossed the threshold into the House of God and closed the door behind him. Light spilled into the sanctuary for just a moment and then it was swallowed by shadows. Heavy footfalls echoed through the empty sanctuary, touching the high places where only the sound of rousing hymns had ever reached before.

"Corbett?" said the interloper. "Are you here?"

There was no answer from the gathering gloom.

"Where are you Boston Corbett?"

Blood stained the floorboards, but the shadows concealed the place where Corbett's life has spilled out. The footfalls grew closer to the center of the sanctuary. They passed it. The interloper had no idea that the man who shot John Wilkes Booth was crouching down between two pews, clutching a kerosene lantern to his belly.

Corbett listened as the interloper approached, picturing the man's every movement in his mind. This man in the uniform of a soldier was no mortal, but a serpent—a demon that served the Society of the Cincinnati. This Hellspawn had come to steal Corbett's soul, but that wasn't going to happen. Boston Corbett had dealt with this ilk before and he knew exactly how to send this demon back to the pits of Hell.

When the man passed by, his heavy boots thudding on the floor, Corbett rose up behind him as silent as shadow. He hoisted the lantern over his head and smashed it against the interloper's skull. The demon screamed as oil ran down his face and into his eyes. Corbett remained calm. He reached into his pocket and produced a box of matches. He flicked one to life with his his fingernail and then tossed it onto the interloper.

The sound of agonized shrieks that emanated from the demon's throat did not give Boston Corbett any pleasure. He had killed before and might be forced to do so again, but he did it out of necessity. He was a man of peace and love, but he did what was necessary to preserve his own life. He felt nothing as the interloper rushed past him, crashed into a row of pews, and then sank to the floor in a burning, screaming pile.

The fire of Hell, fueled by burning oil, licked up all around him and smoke was vomiting from the wretched husk that was once a man. Corbett knew that he must flee this place before he was consumed, but a lung full of smoke sent him into a fit of coughing that nearly killed him. He had lost so much blood already and he was beginning to feel light headed. He turned toward the door and saw it open wide. He saw a figure silhouetted against the flames.

"Lord Jesus," Corbett said. "Please deliver me from this..."

The silhouetted figured took a step back, holding the door open wide. "Come on," he shouted. "Run!"

Corbett ran for his life. He passed through the door and into the wide world outside. He fell to the ground and began rolling back and forth in the grass.

He was coughing so hard that he couldn't breath, and it felt like his organs were about to rupture. Was this the end? he wondered. Was he going to die here with the truth about the Society of the Cincinnati untold?

The man who shot John Wilkes Booth lay back in the grass, his body ruined and his breath coming in ragged gasps. He opened his eyes and looked up into the face of his savior. The face was familiar, but it was not Jesus Christ who leaned over him. Boston Corbett knew this man, and that realization filled him with horror.

"You!"

The soldier known as Price smiled a wicked smile. "Hello Thomas. I see that you remember me."

Memories of a year of torture at the hands of this man flooded into Corbett's mind. Price was his inquisitor at the Topeka State Hospital—the man that pried off his fingernails and pried open his mind with a thousand tortures worse than death. He wanted to know about Booth.

"Tell me about John Wilkes Booth," Price said.

"I never saw him before that day when I killed him," said Corbett.

"No, you were conditioned together by the Society of the Cincinnati," said Price.

It sounded wrong, but Corbett found himself agreeing anyway, like an actor mindlessly repeating his lines for a stage play. "Booth served the Society. He was their agent. He murdered Lincoln on their orders."

"You have learned your lessons well," Price said. "You are a good and faithful servant and the Father and the Son and the Holy Ghost commend you for your work."

Corbett wept. He knew that this was wrong, that his memories were being twisted, but he could do nothing. He was lying on the grass in front of the church and simultaneously he was lying on his cot back at the Topeka State Hospital. He wasn't sure if he was dead or alive.

"Have you located the Society's master in this town?"

"Yes."

"Tell me his name." Price bared his teeth as he spoke.

Corbett struggled to protect the name, but he could not. "Jeremy Farnum," he said.

Price smiled warmly. "Well done, thou good and faithful servant."

Corbett lay back in the grass, coughing violently. Price stood, drew his pistol, and fired a single shot into Corbett's head. The man who shot John Wilkes Booth felt nothing and for just an instant he understood what had happened. The web of lies unraveled before his eyes and the truth became clear. What is truth, he thought. And then Boston Corbett died.

The church was burning and thick smoke billowing into the night sky when Webb and Farnum came on the scene. The sight filled the editor with dread. It was as if the secret cabals that operated in the shadows had murdered God himself. He supposed that they did, if the Scriptures could be believed. Sarah certainly believed them, and she always wanted him to kneel down beside her and worship the God of the Bible. He could never bring himself to do so when she was alive, and he resented God for letting her die. But now...

There was a man in an Army uniform praying over a body; he rose as soon as the surrey came into view.

"The Army has been following us ever since Corbett escaped," Webb said. "Looks like they found him first."

Farnum glared at him. "If that's the case, you're going to come to regret the incidents of the past few days."

Webb already regretted all of it. He had spent years chasing after shadows while Abby needed a father. His obsession had wounded Elizabeth McLarty, the kindest woman Webb had ever known save for his lost Sarah. And it had cost those soldiers back in Topeka their lives. And what had he gained? A story? Nothing mattered now except Abby, and if that dead body was Corbett, as Webb feared, his hopes were dashed.

The soldier had his pistol drawn as soon as the surrey pulled up in front of the church. He had a round face and a piggish nose that turned up at the end. He stared at them for a moment and then a smile spread across his face. "Mister Webb," said the soldier. He turned his attention to the man in white. "And does that make you Mister Farnum?"

"It does. And you are..."

"Augustus Price. Colonel in the United States Army and brother in the Society of Jesus."

"A Jesuit." The venom in Farnum's voice was unmistakable.

"Yes," said Price. "I have traveled many miles and gone through great trouble to arrange this meeting Mister Farnum."

The story that Corbett told in the doctor's office back in Topeka came ringing into Webb's mind. *There are three infernal organizations vying for power in this nation. The Freemasons... The Skull and Bones Society... and the Society of the Cincinnati.* That seemed so right to Webb at the time, but what if that was a lie. What if there was another secret society Corbett had left out? Webb had come across many inferences to the Jesuit Order during his years on the *Paradise Ledger*. Was it possible that they had something to do with the Lincoln Assassination?

"Farnum," said Webb. "Tell me the truth, was Booth a member of your Society?"

"No," Farnum said.

Price's smile widened. "Your late friend Mister Corbett told you that he and Booth were trained together by the Society of the Cincinnati. Is that right? That was a memory that I implanted in his mind."

"For what purpose?" Farnum demanded.

"For *this* purpose," said Price. "My superiors conceived of a plan to use your assassin against you. Corbett came into our custody in Topeka, and we spent more than a year reconditioning him so that he would lead us to you Mister Farnum."

"Me?"

"The master of the Society of the Cincinnati in Colorado. You're quite a prize, Mister Farnum." He waved his gun at the men in the surrey. "Why don't you step down here."

Farnum obeyed.

"You too Mister Webb."

Webb climbed down from the surrey, wondering whom Price was going to murder first.

"The both of you look like Hell. Did you get in a fight?"

Webb and Farnum exchanged a look but said not a word.

"What now?" Farnum asked. "Will you murder me right here in cold blood or haul me back to your Superior General like a prisoner in chains?"

"He will be most interested to speak with you," said Price. He turned his attention to Webb. "Unfortunately, Mister Webb, you will not be accompanying us on the trip back east."

The colonel raised his weapon, and Webb closed his eyes as he prepared for the bullet that would end his life. His hopes of rescuing Abby and making Elizabeth his wife would never come to pass. He heard the hammer click as Price pulled it back.

"Not so fast," came a familiar voice.

Webb opened his eyes and saw Ranse standing behind the colonel, a carbine rifle poised at his shoulder. He had one eye closed and the other trained down the rifle's sights. Ranse was a damned good shot, and Webb had no doubt that if his friend pulled the trigger he would put Colonel Price in his grave.

"What are you doing, Nigger?" Price tried to sound calm, but Webb could detect the anger boiling beneath his words.

"I'm protecting my friend," Ranse said.

The sound of aggravated shouts came from the direction of town, and everyone looked to see the people of Paradise rushing toward the burning church. They would be here in just a minute.

"You're messing around with trouble the likes of which you've never seen."

"I've known trouble my whole life, and I've known Mister Webb for fifteen years. And I like Joshua a whole lot more. Now drop your gun."

Price remained motionless, his gun still pointed at Webb. "I don't think you have it in you," he said. "To shoot a man down like a dog."

"People like you have been underestimating me my entire life," said Ranse. "You ain't the first and you sure as Hell won't be the last. Now I'm gonna say it again... drop your gun."

Price glared viciously at Ranse and then tossed his pistol into the dirt. "You had best shoot me," he said, "because if you don't..."

The mob arrived, some toting buckets of water, but every soul in town knew as soon as they saw the flames that their little church was lost. Smoke was pouring from the windows and the roof was beginning to collapse. Sheriff Watters appeared out of the crowd, took one look at Ranse holding a gun on three white men, and immediately drew his gun.

"What the Hell is going on here?" he demanded.

"Sheriff," said Price, "the colored folks in your town don't seem to know their place in the world."

Watters pulled back the hammer on his pistol. "Ranse, you need to drop that rifle right now."

Ranse slowly moved his finger away from the trigger and dropped his rifle. Webb stood there in the background, watching the whole thing unfold like a scene in a stage play, but whether it was a tragedy or a comedy he couldn't tell. Paradise, for all its flaws, was a nice town and trouble rarely rolled in on the afternoon train. Sheriff Watters seldom had trouble cross his path, but here it was and he was going to have to deal with it.

"You want to tell me what's going on, Colonel?"

Price motioned to Corbett's body, lying dead in the grass. "The fugitive I was searching for the other day, I found him here, but not before he burned down your church. I lost one of my men trying to apprehend him."

"Why was Ranse holding a gun on you, Mister?"

Price looked over at Farnum and smiled sardonically. "I'm sure it was all a misunderstanding. Wouldn't you agree Mister Farnum?"

The man in white nodded his head. "A misunderstanding. Yes."

"Do you have any idea why he burned our town church to the ground?"

The colonel shrugged. "He was a madman. Who can say what twisted thoughts went through his mind."

Watters was clearly frustrated, but Farnum and Price had constructed a lie with only a brief look passing between them. Whatever their differences, these men clearly wanted to keep hidden the secret societies that they represented. Finally, the sheriff turned to Webb.

"What about you, Mister Webb? Do you have anything to add?"

Webb looked at the charred remains of Boston Corbett. All of this trouble began with a letter, and Webb still didn't know if he was ever going to see Abby again. A part of him, the part that believed in justice and the goodness of his fellow man, wanted to tell the sheriff the whole truth. But what would happen if he did? He was known to the people of Paradise as a lunatic, not much better than Corbett, and Watters was likely to roll his eyes if Webb unveiled exactly what had happened here. It was written in the Holy Bible that the truth shall make you free, but what about Abby? What about Boston Corbett?

"A misunderstanding," said Webb. "I thought Mister Corbett could provide some insight into the

Lincoln Assassination, but as Colonel Price just said, he was a madman."

Watters reset the hammer on his pistol and then placed his gun back into its holster. He adjusted his Stetson. The townsfolk had gathered around the scene and they were demanding answers about the church. The sheriff had his hands full and gave no more attention to the participants in the little showdown that had nearly unfolded in his town.

Price turned to Farnum as soon as the sheriff was gone. "I'd suggest that you get your life in order," he said. "We know who you are now, and we could come for you at any time." He shifted his attention to Ranse. "And you, Nigger, if I ever see you again I'll put a rope around your neck."

Ranse's eyes narrowed as he bent down to retrieve his rifle. He said nothing, but the look on his face spoke volumes. Webb wished that things could be different in this land of supposed freedom, but he didn't suppose that it ever would be.

The colonel didn't say a word to Webb. He picked up his gun, slipped it into its holster, and then disappeared into the crowd. That left Webb, Farnum and Ranse standing together on the edge of the crowd.

"What now?" Webb asked. "You're holding all the cards, Farnum."

Farnum looked momentarily confused. He was likely thinking about his own situation and not the fact that Abby was locked away in his attic. "It was a mistake to talk to Boston Corbett. What's going on here is bigger than that rag you call a newspaper."

"Tell me something I don't know."

"Tell me, what are you planning to print in your newspaper, Mister Webb?"

Welcome to Paradise, Webb thought. *The land of the free and the home of the brave. Where we've lost faith in the republic that our fathers died for. Now a handful of men behind closed doors decide the fate of millions. These villains who kill in plain sight and would do anything to retain power.* He could print the truth and expose the Jesuit Order and the Society of the Cincinnati, but people didn't want the truth. They wanted dogma and rhetoric. They didn't care about the truth.

"I don't know," he said at last.

"Your daughter is alive, and unharmed," Farnum said. "I'll return her to you and guarantee her safety, so long as our secrets are never exposed."

"And if I print the truth?"

Farnum's eyes narrowed. "I'll rape her and kill her while you watch."

Webb grimaced. He had no choice but to make a deal with the devil. "I'll print whatever you want me to print if it means you'll return my girl."

Farnum nodded solemnly. "Boston Corbett escaped from an asylum in Topeka," he said, "and he was never seen again. He rode off into the sunset. Print a legend, Mister Webb, and someday it will become fact. Do we have an agreement?"

"We do."

They shook hands and Webb wanted to scream. The man in white tipped his hat at Ranse and then walked away.

Webb watched him go, hating himself for what he was about to do but willing to do it just the same. He would do anything to save his girl, even if it meant compromising his ideals.

"You alright Joshua?" Ranse asked.

"Not really," said Webb, "but I'll learn to live with it."

★ ★ ★ CHAPTER 15 ★ ★ ★
TRUTH AND LEGENDS

The strange tale of Boston Corbett didn't even end up on the front page of the *Paradise Ledger*. A company of soldiers were ambushed outside of Paradise by a band of outlaws. They were killed, to a man, including their commanding officer, Colonel Augustus Price. Webb had his suspicions that those outlaws were none other than Jeremy Farnum's cowboys, but he was beyond caring at this point. He wanted his daughter back, and if it meant sacrificing his journalistic integrity, he was willing to do that. There was nothing he wouldn't sacrifice to bring Abby back home.

According to the story in the *Paradise Ledger*, Boston Corbett escaped from an asylum in Topeka, Kansas and was last seen heading toward Mexico. There was no mention of the Society of the Cincinnati or the Jesuit Order. There was no mention of the body buried in an unmarked grave near the ruins of a church that once stood in Paradise, Colorado.

Who could say if the truth would ever be told? He typed out his own account of the story and left it in a safe deposit box in the Paradise Bank. Perhaps, at some future time, the people of this great nation would be ready for the truth. Or perhaps the pages would moulder there forever, and the lie would become legend, and the legend become truth. As far as Joshua Webb was concerned, it didn't matter either way.

When the papers were printed and the ink was still drying, Webb returned to his little house on the outskirts of town. The place felt empty with Abby gone. He knew that he should have gone out to see Elizabeth, but he just had to be alone now. He stripped off his clothes, wearing nothing but a red union suit, and lay down in his bed. He was hungry, but not hungry enough to cook. It felt wrong to him, moving on with his life with his girl missing. As bad as it had been after Sarah died, this was worse. Much worse.

Webb laced his fingers behind his head and stared up at the ceiling. "Oh God," he said to the darkness. "Are you there? I'm not much of a praying man, I know... God, I'm so worried about my Abby. Please, please I'm begging you, bring her back safe. I want to change my life. I want to be the father that she deserves. Instead I brought all this trouble because of my foolishness."

He closed his eyes. He opened them.

"God, I feel so terrible about Elizabeth. I'm in love with her, but I'm afraid she'll never be able to forgive me for what happened. I'm so sorry... I..."

"Wake up!"

Webb's eyes popped open. He wasn't even aware that he had fallen asleep. The room was flickering with the orange light of a kerosene lamp. He sat up and saw half a dozen black-robed figures standing around his bed. They wore pointed hoods with slits cut out for their eyes, and a long-necked eagle embroidered over their hearts. Webb recognized it at once as the insignia of the Society of the Cincinnati.

"Where's Abby?" Webb demanded.

"She's outside," said one of the hooded figures. Webb recognized the voice at once; it was Jeremy Farnum.

"I want to see her."

"In a minute. I want to talk to you first."

Webb peered up at the imposing figure. He was hopelessly outnumbered, but he didn't think Farnum and his cronies wanted to hurt him. They had done that already. They broke him like a wild mustang, but if Webb had learned anything during the course of the past few days, it was that players like Farnum and the Society always had one more shovel full of coals to heap on the fire.

"Say what you have to say, and then take me to my daughter."

"You set out to prove that there was a conspiracy surrounding the murder of Abraham Lincoln," said Farnum. "You wanted to open up people's eyes and show them the truth about this great nation of ours. You wanted to change the world. Am I wrong?"

Webb shook his head. "You're not wrong."

"Here's the thing, it is a fool's hope that men can ever change. They will not. They cannot. The entire political system of this nation is a ruse, Mister Webb. A farse. The people choosing their leader from a pool of qualified candidates... rubbish. There are an elite few that shape the history of the world with the stroke of a pen. My superiors in the Society of the Cincinnati, they do what they think is best for the greater good. I'm sure Colonel Price and the members of his order would say the same."

"If Colonel Price were still alive," Webb added.

There was a sound beneath Farnum's hood that might have been a chuckle. "The true leaders of the world, they let you see only what they want you to see, Mister Webb. Everything else is distraction and illusion. Two political parties? Yet no matter which ones sits in the Oval Office, the agenda of an enlightened few moves forward. And you and I... we are pawns to move around the chess board and to be sacrificed at will. Only pawns."

"You're not telling me anything that I haven't figured out already," said Webb. "I'd take back everything that has happened since I got Corbett's first letter if I could." He didn't say it out loud, but he would have taken back everything that had happened since Sarah died as well. He had every opportunity in the world, yet he couldn't help sliding down into every slough of despond that crossed his path.

"I'm telling you these things," Farnum said, "because I want you to remember these events should you ever feel tempted to retract your story about Boston Corbett."

"Why does Corbett matter so much to you? You tortured that poor man into madness."

Farnum sighed beneath his hood. "Because he was one of our own, and we loved him. Now, let's go see your daughter."

Webb followed the hooded men into the night. The sky was perfectly clear, and the heavens were overflowing with stars too numerous to count. There was a wagon parked in front of the house, and another black-robed figure sitting in the driver's seat. Four tall horses stamped and nickered in place before the wagon. Webb's legs nearly buckled beneath him as they led him outside. It felt like he was being led to his own hearse, and in fact there was a coffin in the back of the wagon.

They approached the coffin in silence, the feeling growing heavier with every step that Farnum had betrayed his end of the deal. Webb wasn't sure what he would do if they opened that box and Abby was lying there, dead. He felt his calm slipping and forced himself to put one foot in front of the other.

Several of the black-robed men reached over the edges of the wagon and lifted out the coffin. They were gruesome pall bearers, marching three by three and setting the box down in the dewy grass. Farnum took Webb by the shoulder and led him to the place where the coffin lay.

"Go on," he said, "open it."

Webb bent down, jammed his fingers under the lid, and heaved open the coffin. Abby was inside, her hands folded over her chest like the hands of a corpse. She was so pale... so beautiful. Webb's heart shattered the moment he looked at her.

"Abby? Oh my God."

Abby's eyes popped open. "Papa?" She sat up and threw her arms around him.

Webb felt tears spilling down his cheeks, but he didn't care. His heart was restored the instant that he heard his daughter's voice. They were together again, and he was never going to let anything come between them again. He tried to speak, but he was so overcome with emotion that the words got stuck in his throat.

Farnum climbed into the bed of the wagon; his confederates gathered around him as they prepared to depart. "You have your girl," he said, "and you have your life. But be warned, Mister Webb, both could be snatched away from you in an instant." He signaled the driver and the wagon pulled away into the night.

When they were gone, when father and daughter were finally alone, Abby leaned against her father and sobbed. Webb held her for a long time, petting her hair and not saying a word as his girl let out all of the emotion that was bottled up inside her.

"Did they hurt you?" Webb asked.

"No. Scared me awful bad, but they didn't hurt me. I saw what they did to you, Papa. I... I'm so sorry."

"I'm fine." He held her close but she pulled away.

"Is Elizabeth..."

"That young man... Avery. He raped her and gouged out her eye."

Abby's face tightened with grief, and though her body was wracked with sobs, no more tears spilled down her cheeks.

"Where is she?"

"At the Shinbone place in Browntown."

"What's she doing there?"

"I wasn't sure if I could trust Doc Hostetler," said Webb. "To be honest, I'm not sure if I'll ever trust anyone again."

"She loves you," Abby said. "Did you know that?"

"Elizabeth? Yeah, I know. And now that I know you're safe I'm going to do something I should have done a long time ago."

"What's that?"

"I'm going to ask her to marry me."

Elizabeth McLarty looked at herself in the mirror and cringed. There was a gaping hole in her face where her left eye should have been.

"You just gotta give it time," said Mercy. "It'll close up and you can wear..."

"You know what time means to a woman," said the widow. "Even before this happened I didn't exactly have suitors lining up to ask me to dance. And now..." she shook her head, trying to chase away the memories of the nightmare she had endured. Ranse Shinbone had returned the day before and told all about what had transpired out to the church. Boston Corbett was dead and Joshua's big story had unraveled before his eyes. Would he want her now that Avery had taken her and used her like a whore?

"Mister Webb is waiting," said Mercy. "He looks awfully handsome without that beard."

Elizabeth feigned a smile. She didn't want to see Joshua or anyone else. She would have been happy to crawl into a cave and die. What was life anyway but sorrow stacked upon sorrow? She thought about Charles and how empty she felt for years after he died. She was all alone in the world, and she was going to be alone until they laid her in the ground beside her late husband.

"I'm going to send him in. Are you ready?"

"Sure. Fine." Elizabeth turned her head away from the door so that her wound would not be the first thing Joshua saw. Her heart was sick and she felt weak all over.

Mercy left the room and, a moment later, Joshua and Abby appeared in the doorway. The widow smiled in spite of everything at the site of the girl. She had worried so for her young friend, and to see her alive again was a joy. Abby darted across the room and threw her arms around the widow. There was nothing for Elizabeth to do but to hug her back.

"I'm so happy to see you, said Abby.

Elizabeth stroked the girl's hair. "Me too," she whispered.

Joshua took a step closer and offered a shy smile. He did look handsome without that beard, but Elizabeth kept her eyes averted. She didn't want him gawking at her.

"Hello Elizabeth."

"Hello Joshua."

"I brought you these." He handed her a bouquet of wildflowers. Daisies and Black-eyed Susans.

"They're beautiful," she said, focusing her attention on the flowers so she wouldn't have to look up.

"Elizabeth," said Webb, "I want to apologize for putting you in harm's way. I was a fool. I never should have answered those letters."

She was going to tell him that it was all right, but she couldn't bring herself to tell the lie.

"I've been thinking a lot these past few days," he continued, "about my life here in Paradise and all the time I've wasted chasing ghosts and shadows. The only part of the work that's really meant anything to me was the time I spent with you."

Elizabeth's heart trembled at the words—words she had longed to hear for so long. But she probably misunderstood his meaning, she knew that.

"I don't know if it was my pride or what it was that kept me running all over the country, chasing down every conspiracy that reared its ugly head. But I'm not going to do it anymore."

"You're not?"

He shook his head emphatically. "From now on the *Paradise Ledger* is strictly a traditional newspaper. Local news and stories of interest, that's it. I'm through with wandering in the darkness."

Elizabeth smiled meekly and nodded her head. "That's good. I'm happy for you."

"There's something else," he said.

The widow caught a glance between father and daughter in her peripheral vision. "What's that?"

Joshua knelt down beside the bed and took Elizabeth by the hand. "Will you look at me," he said.

"Joshua, I..."

"Please?"

"I can't. I'm so ugly now."

He touched her on the cheek and gently moved her head so that he could see her wound. "You will never be ugly to me, Elizabeth."

She started to cry, she couldn't help herself. "Joshua, please..."

"Elizabeth, it was my obsession with conspiracies that put you and Abby in harm's way. It was my obsession that put you here. I know that apologizing will never undo what's been done, but I *am* sorry. I don't deserve your love Elizabeth, but I would be honored to be your husband if you would have me."

She tried to speak but the words would not form. She nodded her head slowly as Joshua, her fiancé, wrapped her in a warm embrace. When his lips met hers she felt for the first time that everything was going to be all right. Certainly she would have troubles as the years went on, but the burden that had weighed on her shoulders ever since Charles died was finally lifted. Abby stepped forward and threw her arms around the pair. They were, at long last, what they should have been all along–a family.

Webb knelt by his first wife's grave on the windy hilltop overlooking his homestead. He laid a bouquet of flowers by her headstone and lovingly touched the letters of her name with the tips of his fingers.

"Sarah," he said, "I wanted to tell you some of the things that have been going on around here since you went away. I know that I haven't been up to see you very often… frankly, it breaks my heart to come to this place. I… I've let you down, my darling. I've failed."

He felt tears brimming in his eyes but they did not overflow. It might have brought him some comfort to cry, but he would not or could not. Webb let out a sigh and then continued.

"Our sweet girl… she nearly died because of my pride and my obsession. I've spent so much time chasing shadows, and all I've got to show for it is wasted years. Wasted time."

He thought about a trip to Harpers Ferry he and Abby had taken many years before. How might things have been different if he seized that opportunity to lay this madness to rest? Instead he put in long hours at his office while his girl grew a little bit older every day. She wasn't his little girl anymore, but nearly a woman grown. That time was lost and he could never get it back.

"I found myself praying to your Jesus these past few days because I didn't know who else to turn to. I bet you never thought you would hear me say that. Remember all those Sundays you asked me to come to church and I found a reason not to go? Remember all those mornings you asked me to pray with you?"

Webb stared up into the sky, picturing the creator of the universe looking down at him. "It was never that I didn't believe in God," he said. "I grew up washed in the blood of the lamb just like everybody else in my family, but after the Army, after Washita, I came to believe that God hated me because of the things I had done. Can you understand that? I thought I was cursed, and that was the reason that you..."

His heart tightened in a spasm of physical pain.

"I don't know if this is foolish," he said, "but I feel like God took you away to punish me. I've done some terrible things in my life, Sarah. Things that make me feel ashamed to look in a mirror. My sin is ever before me... King David said that a long time ago, and that's exactly how I feel now. I've buried that feeling in my work, but now I see that I was wretched, and miserable, and poor, and blind, and naked."

Webb sat in silence for several minutes, listening to the sound of the wind on the mountains and, in the woods, a murder of crows scolding a bird of prey. His heart was laid bare to the one person with whom he could always be totally honest. Sarah was a good woman, better than he deserved, and he would love her until the day he died. But Abby needed a mother and he needed someone to share his life.

"I want you to know that I'm going to make a change," he said at last. "The Ledger... I'm done with secret societies and conspiracy theories. I'm through chasing ghosts. What could seizing hold of any of those things ever bring me but sorrow? From now on I'm putting Abby first. For however long I've still got her, I'm going to treat her like something precious... like one of these flowers. And I hope you can understand that I'm finally going to move on with my life. I love you as much now as I did on the day you were my bride, but I can't live in the past anymore. I've fallen in love with a good woman and she cares for Abby like she's her own daughter. We're going to be married, but that doesn't mean I'm going to forget you or love you any less. I just... oh Sarah, I've felt so alone since you went away... so scared and alone. The whole world is wrong and there's nothing we can do about it. Nothing. We just go through the motions, one step at a time, one step closer to eternity. Perhaps it's like it says in the Bible, I don't know. Abby is alive and so is Elizabeth, and I can't look at that as a coincidence. But the world is brimming with evil that can never be overcome. I... I just want to live in peace and take care of my family. I just want you to understand… I know you do. I know you can hear me somewhere, Sarah. I love you, and I always will."

The tears finally came now, and though they were few, Webb felt his burden lifted once they were wept. He wiped his eyes with the back of his sleeve and smiled at Sarah's grave. For all he knew, her ghost might be lingering there watching him.

"I have to go now," he said. "I'll be back, but maybe not for a while." He touched her name one last time with the tips of his fingers and whispered, "goodbye."

Joshua Webb walked back down the hill toward his homestead, toward Abby and Elizabeth and all of the years of joy and sorrow that awaited him there. The whole world was wrong, but come Hell or high water, he was going to do his best to make this little piece of it into something good.

THE END

CANCELED
★ ★ ★ AN AUTHOR'S NOTE ★ ★ ★

This story has been through some hard times.

The Man Who Shot John Wilkes Booth was originally conceived as a comic book. It was, once upon a time, under contract with a medium-sized comic book publisher whose name I cannot reveal. Unfortunately, the artist that was attached to the project vanished (much like Boston Corbett did in real life) and I was left with a handful of beautifully illustrated pages (you can see some of them sprinkled throughout this book) and a project that was never going to make it to the press.

What to do? What to do?

In the years since I filed away the scripts for *The Man Who Shot John Wilkes Booth*, the indie publishing revolution, or as I like to call it, outlaw publishing, suddenly happened. I got my toes wet with a short story called *The Bell Curse* set in the World of Kurt Vonnegut, and then plunged in headfirst with a short novel called *Legendarium*, co-written with Michael Bunker. That book was a hit and put me on the map. I needed a follow-up story and I needed it quick.

So there I was, with a tale that was fully researched, fully outlined, and fully scripted, that was never going to be a comic book. The logical choice was to turn it into a novel. The characters came right back to me, and the book launched my career as a solo novelist. I moved on, wrote a supernatural horror novel called *The Bleak December*, a sequel to *Legendarium* called *Legendarium: The Wrath Of Bob*, and then a space opera trilogy called *Starship Gilead* that was set to launch in March 2022. All the while, *The Man Who Shot John Wilkes Booth* was there on my back list, waiting for new readers who stumbled across my work.

And then something happened that changed my life.

It was a Saturday night in January 2022. I was about to turn in when I stupidly decided to check my email before bed. I should have left that damned phone sitting on the charger. Instead, I saw an email from Amazon KDP.

KDP (Kindle Direct Publishing) is a service provided by Amazon that allows authors to publish on their platform. There are other platforms to sell ebooks, but if you want to be part of Kindle Unlimited, a subscription service that gives you access to unlimited ebooks, then KDP is your **only** avenue. Kindle Unlimited is where the money is. A great majority of readers use the service to read as many ebooks as they want. There are people out there that read a book a day, and authors get paid by the page-read.

The email accused me of having multiple KDP accounts, which is a violation of Amazon's terms of service. My KDP account was terminated and I was forbidden from ever opening another one.

The only problem was, I didn't have multiple KDP accounts. I had been using the same account since I started self-publishing in 2014 and I'd never opened a second one. There was no reason to. It just didn't make any sense.

I figured this must be a bot error or something, but every time I tried to appeal to the powers that be, I was shut down. Was there more to the story? Was there something in one of my books that somebody didn't like? Normally when someone gets canceled they are publicly crucified on Twitter, but that didn't happen to me. It was just like I had never existed. I felt like John Proctor in *The Crucible*. "I've given you my soul, but leave me my name." I felt like Winston Smith in *1984*. I watched in sick horror as my books were shoved into the memory hole and burnt up.

My protests fell on deaf ears.

Amazon wasn't interested in hearing my side of the story. I was guilty until proven innocent, and the punishment was the termination of my self-publishing career. The literary outlaw was on the gallows and Jeff Bezos was about to drop the noose.

Surely something could be done, right? This is Amazon, the company that started the self-publishing boom. The company that put the gatekeepers on notice. They wouldn't just ignore reason would they?

They would.

Amazon doesn't care about authors. Amazon doesn't care about right and wrong. Amazon cares about making money. They're not interested in paying someone to look into their mistakes. They just don't care.

My first three published stories were set in the *Star Trek* universe. They appear in the *Star Trek: Strange New Worlds IV, Star Trek: Strange New Worlds*

08, and *Star Trek Deep Space Nine: Prophecy and Change* anthologies. I've been a Trekkie all my life, and I hear that Jeff Bezos is a Trekkie as well. He paid to be in *Star Trek Beyond*. He put William Shatner in space. I think he sees himself as a Zephram Cochran type of character, but I don't see him that way at all. If Bezos is like anyone in the Star Trek universe he's Grand Nagus Zek, a man who is rich beyond his wildest dreams, but that has no moral obligation to do what is right. He doesn't know my name. My name doesn't matter. The truth about this situation doesn't matter. I'm supposed to just shut up and go away. Amazon destroyed my career and my dreams and I didn't even get to talk to a person on the phone. I got canceled with a form letter.

Bezos canceled my writing career two months before I was set to launch a new series.

Two months. What was I supposed to do?

I connected with some publisher friends of mine at Aethon Books, and upon their advice I scrubbed my name from *Starship Gilead* and published the series under a pen name, John Graves. The first book is out now, and it's doing well. It's too bad that folks who read it have no idea about all the other books I wrote. Normally the Amazon algorithm will show those books to new readers, but not anymore. I'm almost fifty years old and I have to start all over with a new name.

Thank God for Draft2Digital and Ingram Spark. At least I can get this book and my other titles back on the market. I don't know how they will do without Kindle Unlimited, but these books are my legacy. My name isn't my legacy anymore, Amazon took that from me.

So that's the long story of *The Man Who Shot John Wilkes Booth*—how it came to be and how it ended up in your hands. I thank you for reading, and for following me out here into the frontier. I got knocked off my horse and spent some time staring up at the sky. There were buzzards circling overhead. I thought I was done for, but my wife and my kids and my friends pulled me back up on my feet and now I'm back in the saddle again. Jeff Bezos doesn't want you to read this book, but you and me, we're outlaws and we don't give a shit what Bezos wants. We read what we want, and that's what makes us literary outlaws.

Now let's ride.

Kevin G. Summers
April 12, 2022

★ ★ ★ BONUS STORY ★ ★ ★

THE PARABLE OF THE SOWER

BY KEVIN G. SUMMERS AND JAMES HALE

THE PARABLE OF THE SOWER was originally printed out as an "ashcan" and handed out to prospective publishers at comic book conventions. This story is set before the events of THE MAN WHO SHOT JOHN WILKES BOOTH and is referenced briefly in the novel.

THE
Paradise Ledger
PRESENTS
The PARABLE of The SOWER

By Kevin G. Summers And James Hale

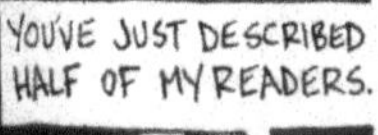

WE LIVED ON MY FATHERS OLD PLANTATION JUST EAST OF HERE. EIGHTEEN-HUNDRED ACRES OF SUGARCANE RIGHT ON THE MISSISSIPPI. IT WAS SIMPLY BREATHTAKING.
IT WAS THE HAPPIEST TIME IN MY LIFE. MY HUSBAND, EDWARD, AND ME, AND OUR THREE BOYS — WE HAD EVERYTHING A FAMILY COULD DESIRE UNTIL THAT... THAT NIGGER LOVER STARTED HIS WAR.
OUR OLDEST, ROBERT, DIED FIGHTING THE YANKEES. THEN WE WERE TOLD WE HAD TO FREE OUR SLAVES... I THOUGHT WE WERE RUINED.

BUT EDWARD HAD A PLAN. HE HEARD ABOUT THESE WORKERS THEY HAVE DOWN IN HAITI, SO HE HIRED THIS VOODOO WOMAN FROM NAWLINS TO DELIVER US A NEW CROP OF SLAVES.
BUT THESE SLAVES...
...I DON'T KNOW HOW, BUT THAT WITCH USED HER VOODOO MAGIC TO RAISE UP THE DEAD.

SUDDENLY WE HAD MONEY AGAIN. I WAS SO HAPPY I TOOK A TRIP TO BATON ROUGE TO VISIT MY SISTER. THAT WAS IN THE SUMMER OF '68.

NOW YOU REMEMBER, GHEDA, SO LONG AS YOU TAKE CARE AH ME I'LL TAKE CARE AH YOU. I DON'T KNOW WHAT I WOULD'VE DONE WITHOUT THOSE...
...WORKERS YOU CONJURED UP FOR ME.

GOODNIGHT, GHEDA. MAKE SURE BREAKFAST IS ON THE TABLE WHEN I GET UP.

THE NEXT MORNING...
TI BON ANGE.

TI BON ANGE

TOUYE...
...OU METRIZE.

YOUR MOTHER SENDS
HER LOVE AND WANTS ME
TO REMIND YOU...

krrrreeeaaak

WHAT WAS THAT?

PROBABLY
JUST MY
IMAGINATION...

KRAKK
KRAKK
KRAKK
AAAAHHH!

RETURN TO YOUR ENDLESS SLEEP.
YOU HAVE EARNED YOUR REST, MY BROTHERS.
SHE WAS WAITING FOR ME WHEN I RETURNED HOME.

GHEDA TOLD ME EVERTHING SHE HAD DONE... THAT EDWARD HAD DONE.
WHY DID SHE LET YOU LIVE?
TO PUNISH ME. TO REMIND ME OF THAT OLD PROVERB...
FOR WHATSOEVER A MAN SOWETH, THAT SHALL HE ALSO REAP.
THE END

ACKNOWLEDGEMENTS

I owe a debt of thanks to the following people who provided valuable feedback on this story: James Hale, Debby Stapleton, Preston Leigh, Brodie Williams, and Derek Attico. I want to thank Michael Bunker, Nick Cole, and Derek Gilbert for writing such nice blurbs about my book. A kind word from someone you admire goes a long way.

I especially want to thank Steven G. Miller, the world's foremost expert on Boston Corbett, who took me out to breakfast and helped ensure that I was accurate with the character. Everything I got right about Corbett came from Steve, and everything I got wrong... well, that was my fault.